ABIGAIL'S DESIRE

ABIGAIL'S DESIRE

MISTY HALL

Prologue

As I laid there, the life literally draining from my body, it wasn't my life that flashed before my eyes. It was, *"how the fuck did I get to this point?"* My vision was becoming blurry, I was getting colder as I lay on that cold concrete floor. Why did I believe he loved me? Why did I think even for one tiny moment I meant something real to him?

My breath catches a bit in my throat as I inhale. I slowly exhale and find it harder to breathe. I can faintly hear noises in the distance, sounds like shouting, screaming. Fighting. I'm not sure. I'm starting to lose consciousness. My eyes slowly begin to shut, I think to myself *"This is it. This is how it ends. In an abandoned building. Alone. Bleeding out."* I feel a single tear slide down my cheek. I want to reach up to brush it away, but my arms feel so heavy.

When I feel like the end is near, I take one deep breath and let it out slowly. I hear a voice. My name? Is someone talking to me? Is someone there? I'm not sure. I try to open my eyes, but they won't. I try to move but I can't. I suddenly feel arms wrapped around me, shaking me. I can hear them screaming my name, but it sounds muffled. My last thought was *"At least I won't die alone."*

1

Summer was finally ending. Kids were going back to school, and summer activities were winding down. The days were getting shorter and the nights longer. There was a cool crisp to the air at night, and I loved it. The only downside was the fact that I was right smack in the middle of downtown New York City. I sighed as I stared out the window of my small shop, no matter the season, the weather or the time of year; New York City never stopped. It was a constant flow of traffic and people. Day and night.

I missed the fall colors of the countryside. I longed to go upstate and see the trees change color. I knew some trees in Central Park changed with the season, but it wasn't the same. Letting out another sigh, I turned the sign on the door from open to close and locked the deadbolt, before turning to head back to the counter to finish the process of closing. My shop wasn't much, it was small, but it was mine. It held clothing, hats, bags, wallets, belts, jewelry, shoes, candles, herbs, crystals and more. It was kind of a "If you can't find it there, you'll probably find it here" store. I had people laugh at me when I first opened, saying I wouldn't make it. But let me tell you, you slap New York City on anything, and the tourist eat it up. And there are always tourists in New York City.

Once I finished counting my drawer, balancing out the books and making up my deposit to drop off in the morning, I locked the safe and started turning off the lights. I double checked the front doors to make sure they were locked tight. I headed through the back and

2

stopped at the big metal door that led to the alley. I closed my eyes and took a deep breath. Even though I've been living in this city for 8 years, it still terrified me. Especially at night. *"Of course, Theo couldn't show up to give me a drive to my apartment."* I thought to myself as I exhaled and set the alarm before opening the door and pulling it shut behind me and locking it. I glanced around me, as I pulled my jacket closer around me and headed towards the sidewalk still full of people. I glanced at my watch, it was after 9pm and the city was still busy.

After walking for about 10 mins, I finally made it to my apartment building. The main reason I picked this building to live in was the character of it. It was old. Charming. Almost all original stone and woodwork was still alive and beautiful on the inside and outside of this building. It was magnificent. I made my way to my apartment, at the very top of the 4-floor building. I had the corner apartment, which was nice, since it gave me the most natural light with all the windows. It was a small 1 bedroom 1 bathroom apartment. A tiny kitchen, big enough for just me, a decent enough size dining area that was also the living room. My most favorite features of the whole place were all the old, exposed brick walls. The original tiles in the bathroom still looked amazing but showed their age as well. It was the tiny details that most people would ignore. But I loved them.

I did my usual nighttime routine. I ordered pizza, sorted through mail, made a list of things to do the next day, eat the pizza then shower, brush my teeth and sink into my bed staring at the ceiling above me. I'd lay there for an hour or so, trying to sleep. Checking my phone to see if I had any messages from Theo, knowing damn well there wouldn't be any. Sighing deeply, I laid my phone on the nightstand and rolled over on my side, staring out the window. I could hear cars, sirens and people. The city was always busy. It never slept. And as I laid there staring out the window, hoping to sleep, I finally dozed off.

The week went by quickly without much excitement. Theo promised Saturday night he would come pick me up from my shop and we'd go to dinner and then, who knew with Theo. I rolled my eyes just thinking about it. Usually it was just dinner, a boring dinner. Hardly any talking, always on his phone, either texting or excusing himself to have a 10-minute conversation. I groaned out loud before I realized I had a customer in the store. I blushed furiously "I'm so sorry. That...that wasn't towards you." I hurriedly said towards the guy. He gave me a cocked-eyed grin as he moved around the small store that seemed even smaller with him in there "Not a problem, ma'am."

His voice was like velvet. It had an accent attached to it, but it wasn't the New Yorker accent or surrounding. I couldn't quiet put my finger on it. He was fair skinned, dark messy hair, almost pitch black in color. His eyes were bright, yet dark. He was at least 6'2" or more, muscular and toned. He had chiseled features like he was made of marble by the finest hands. When I realized I was staring, I blushed more and shyly smiled and nodded. I turned away to act busy and try to calm myself down. I rolled my eyes at myself and internally groaned as my heart sped up and I went stiff. I could literally feel him behind me at the counter.

I took a deep breath and slowly let it out before turning around. I smiled at the man, I scanned his items without even looking at them, I told him his total and he swiped a card. I bagged his items and handed him the receipt "Thanks for stopping. Have a great night." I said as rushed as anyone could say the words. I felt flustered and I hated it. He let out a chuckle, as he smiled at me. It made my stomach do a flip and my heart go crazy "You do the same, ma'am." He winked and nodded before he grabbed his stuff and walked out of my shop.

I stood there in a daze for a solid 5 mins just thinking about what the hell had just happened. Who was that guy? Why did I feel the way I did? I've seen hundreds of men come through that door looking just as handsome as he did and nothing. Even Theo hardly made me feel that way. *"Theo!"* I panicked as I looked down at my watch, it was after 8:30pm. Theo would be here at 9pm and he would not wait around. If I was even a minute late, he would either bitch about it the entire evening or just leave and no date at all. I hurried to do the daily closing of my shop. I hoped I had no errors, but I figured I could sort them out Sunday if I had to, I rushed to tiny bathroom I had in the back to change quickly into a deep blood red dress, it sparkled like diamonds. It went all the way down to my feet but had a slit clear up to my hip. It was spaghetti strap with a deep dive for the cleavage to show the girls off. I quickly reapplied the simple natural look makeup I had on earlier and added red lipstick to match the dress. I quickly did my hair in an updo of looking like a messy bun, but it was done by a professional for hundreds of dollars. Sighing, as I looked at myself in the mirror, I sometimes wondered what Theo saw in me. Though I thought of myself as beautiful, but I knew there was other women much more beautiful. Even without makeup, I was always told I had that natural look of beauty, which I guess is why I didn't always go heavy with the makeup.

I glanced at my watch and cursed as I saw it was 9pm. I hurried about turning the lights off and locking doors. I set the alarm at the back and walked out the door, locking it behind me. I turned and glanced around, hoping that Theo would come to the alley to get me. I made my way towards the sidewalk at the end and glanced around again. Sighing, I looked at my watch again before looking around. I began making my way around the building to the front, wondering if maybe he parked there. Sure enough, he was. Sighing, I quickly walked towards the car, his driver got out and opened the door for me to get it. I slid into the back of the car where, surprise, Theo was on his phone talking. I instantly got the motion from him to be quiet. I always wondered if maybe he didn't want anyone to know of me. But then again, we wouldn't go into public if that was the case. I settled into the seat as the driver merged into traffic and drove us towards the restaurant. I waited patiently for him to get off the phone, and when he finally did, he didn't even glance at me, speak to me or anything. He went straight to texting on his phone. I quietly sighed to myself and randomly scrolled through my phone and the second I did, I got scolded at for doing so "Why are you always on your phone when you're with me?" Theo asked harshly. I put my phone away and shrugged "I was waiting for you to be done with whatever." I told him.

Theo scoffed and went right back to texting away. Once at the restaurant, the driver opened the door on Theo's side, he got out and I slid out after him. He was at least gentleman enough to hold his hand out to help me get out of the car.

The date went as much as I had expected. He either texted constantly or kept getting up to leave. I was sipping my wine at the end of dinner when my phone went off. I checked it and it was a text from Theo. He had left. My eyes went wide. *"He just fucking leaves?"* At least he paid for dinner before leaving. That was the only plus. I took a big swig of my wine, finishing it off before standing up to leave. I walk outside to hail a taxi and head home.

Once home, I slumped onto the couch, kicking off my stupid heels. I let my long, wavy brown hair down and sigh deeply as I stare up at the ceiling. What was so wrong with me that Theo couldn't even have a real conversation with me? Mostly, why did I keep putting up with it. As I contemplated ways to break up with Theo, I dozed off to sleep on the couch, but the last thing that came to my mind was the man at my shop that made my heart and stomach do somersaults.

2

It had been weeks since I last saw Theo and I ended it with him. I was done being treated like I was below him and not getting the respect I deserved. It still irked me that he left me alone at the restaurant that night and couldn't even come tell me bye, he had someone else do it for him. My mind decided to remind me of why I kept staying with Theo; he was great in bed. He did shower me with love, at times. Even though he was a douchebag, he was a gentleman through and through. I sighed. Wondering if I made a mistake, before I could think more on it, I shook my head "No, Theo was a total ass. He didn't really care about me." I was standing my ground. I've tried dumping him before and he always smoothed talked his way out of it. I was sticking to it this time.

I cleared my head and finished opening the store. I counted the drawers and made sure it was correct. I finished hanging up signs, showing a BOGO FREE on items that I had for a while and just trying to get rid of it. I organized a few things as I made my way to the door and unlocked it. I flipped the sign to open and walked my way back to the counter. I sat on the stool and opened my laptop. I randomly browsed social media, updated my pages for my shop, read some emails and then let out a sigh as I closed my laptop. I checked my watch and groaned. It was definitely a Monday, and it was slooow.

After what seemed like an eternity, the shop became busy. The sale was definitely a hit, especially with the tourists. After a few hours of dealing with non-stop customers, it slowed down. I took a deep breath in and let it out slowly and smiled as I walked around the shop with my tablet, taking note of inventory and things to restock and whether I needed to order more or not. I was happy to see most of all the older items I wanted gone, found new homes. I was ready to get the summer items gone and start putting out fall and Halloween decor and items. I figured by the end of the week I would start rearranging and doing just that. I was just about to turn the sign to close so I could grab a late lunch, when a customer wandered in. "Hi there! Is there anything I could help you with?" I asked the man kindly with a bright smile. The man nonchalantly shrugged his shoulder as he walked about the store. "Oh, not particularly." His New York accent was thick, and I usually didn't get local residents that came in often.

"Well, if you need anything, just let me know." I said in the same kind voice with a smile. He didn't even look at me or acknowledge me. I made my way back to behind the counter, keeping an eye on the man. He was buff, like he hadn't missed a single day of working out at the gym. He was bald, wore a black leather jacket, black undershirt and dark jeans with black boots. There really wasn't anything distinctive about him, really, and he kept texting on his phone, while casually looking at me, but not at me. It gave me chills. *"Just buy something or leave or steal or whatever. Just leave."* I kept thinking to myself. I tried to busy myself aimlessly with stuff behind the counter. I heard the door open again and shut. Then I heard the distinct sound of it locking. That made me go stiff. I looked up at the door and there stood Theo, with 2 more men almost identical to the first guy that came in moments before "Well, this isn't good." I thought to myself.

Theo walked his way up to my counter, no expression on his face to show how he was feeling or thinking. I stood my ground, trying to show no emotion either, even though had a feeling this wasn't a good visit from the man I just dumped.

"Abigail. Abby." He placed his hands on the counter and leaned closer to me. I could smell the scent of him, he always smelled so fresh, like fresh forest air, Musk, fresh pine, woodsy. With just a hint of the cologne he wore, it made my head swirl and my heart pound. It stirred things inside of me and I did my best to hide it, but a grin slowly spread across his face as if he could sense it.

"Theo." I mustered to speak and glad it came out normal. Because I was breaking.

"Abby. We should talk. I've missed you." He leaned in closer to me and by God, I wanted him. I felt myself leaning closer to him, inhaling his scent and wanting to give in to him when a rapid knock sounded on the door. I blinked quickly and pulled back as the four men turned quickly towards the door to see who was stupid enough to disturb them. One of the bald men went to the door to see who it was, he turned back to look directly at me and Theo "It's food delivery." He spoke. Theo looked at me and I smiled sheepishly "I've been very busy today. Late lunch." I shrugged as Theo gestured to the bald man to allow the food guy in.

I was scrambling my brain, because I didn't order food. I didn't even get the chance before Theo's goon came into the store and then he himself barged in and locked the door. As the so-called delivery food guy got closer, I immediately felt my stomach do flips, it was the guy from a few weeks ago. My heart beat crazy, and my stomach did somersaults. He held a brown bag from my favorite Chinese restaurant next door. I could smell the orange chicken and brown rice through the bag and containers. I felt my stomach grumble in response. I did my best to smile, but not too eagerly as he got to the counter "Thanks! I was just about to come over to get it." I said kindly. The man smiled back, as he handed off the bag "My pleasure. Is there anything else you need?" He asked me, I wanted to scream YES! But I didn't know this guy. And I didn't want any kind of harm to come to him "No, thank-you." I told him. He nodded with a smile as he stared at me for a moment before turning to leave. My heart sank. "Damnit. Don't leave... " and almost as if he heard, he stopped before the door and turned towards me "Are you sure you don't need anything else, ma'am?" God, I wanted so badly to tell him to get me help, but with her luck, Theo would just pay off the cops or they would know him, and his family and it would make it worse. I smiled as genuinely as I could "I'm sure.

Thank you." The man nodded before leaving the store. The bald guy by the door locked it and stood right in front of it.

Theo turned to look at me. I frowned at him as I crossed my arms over my chest "I'd kindly like you and your goons to please leave my store. I have nothing to say to you. It's over between us. We are done." I stood my ground. But it was hard. Theo sighed as be racked a hand through his perfectly blonde hair "Abby, we are done when I say we are done." His tone was a bit harsh, and it sent a chill down my spine, especially when he came around the counter and got close behind me. He brushed my hair away from my neck and pressed his face close. I felt him inhale as he rubbed his face against my neck up to my ear "And we are not done." He whispered to me. I felt my body shudder, whether it was from fear or pleasure or both, I wasn't sure. He seemed pleased with himself as he smiled against my neck and lightly kissed it "Be ready by 9pm. Tonight. Wear that black dress I love." He spoke as he pulled away from me and began walking towards the door "I will be at your apartment by 9pm. Be ready." He repeated before his goons unlocked the door and they all left.

I felt myself let out a shaky breath, not realizing I was holding it in. "Damnit!" I thought, as I just stood there for a moment. How did he have such a hold over me? I checked my watch, seeing it was after 3pm. I still hadn't eaten, had inventory to go over and now be ready for Theo. "Fuck.." I muttered quietly to myself then jumped when a voice spoke, I wasn't expecting "Such foul language for a beautiful woman." I didn't even hear someone walk in the door. I looked up to see him again. My heart almost stopped; it definitely skipped a few beats. What was happening to me here? Why was I reacting to two men this way?

"Well. The day I'm having, it's appropriate." I told him with a frown. He stepped closer, never taking his eyes off of me. There was a silence between us for a moment before I finally blinked and looked away "Umm, sorry. I am closing. I haven't eaten and have a million things to get done. If you need to buy, please do it quickly." I rushed the words out as I glanced at him. He just kept staring and it made me melt. He smiled softly at me and nodded "I understand. Just wanted to make sure you were alright." I was almost a puddle on the floor, why was this gorgeous man being so kind? Why did he care what happened to me? "I'm good. Thanks. Just boyfriend drama." I said, waving it off like it was nothing. And when I said boyfriend, the guy looked like I gutted him. And it did something strange to me. I felt...guilty? Shame? "Well, ex-boyfriend. But he won't accept it." I shrugged my shoulders, and the guy seemed a bit better at that.

"Well, an ex that won't accept it can be dangerous." He told me and I nodded agreeing with him. Especially with someone like Theo.

"I'm Nicholas, by the way." He said with a charming smile as he held his hand out to me. I smiled back, as placed my hand in his "Abigail. But everyone just calls me Abby." I had expected a handshake, but instead he pulled my hand up to his mouth and he placed the most tender kiss on my knuckles. I felt things stir inside of him, as he glanced up at me before he stood straight and gently let go of my hand. An emotion flashed across his face and eyes for a moment before it disappeared. Was that hunger, lust? I wasn't sure. But he smiled that most charming smile again "It's nice to meet you, Abby. I will leave. I hope to see you again." I nodded I'm agreement, really hoping so "Nice to meet you too, Nicholas." He turned and left the store. I stood there for a moment before shaking my head and going to lock the door. I turned the sign to close and made my way to the counter. I grabbed the food and tablet and went back to quickly eat and then work on inventory before heading home.

3

⬥

As I got home, I went through the process of showering, doing my hair, and gathering up my outfit. I sighed as I opened my closet door and stared at the black dress towards the back of my closet. It was a gorgeous dress, but I felt like I was exposed wearing it. Frowning, I pulled the dress out and slipped into it. I stared at myself in the full-length mirror, the black dress hugged me in all the right places, it was silk, and went to the floor, with a slit clear up to my hip. It dipped very low in the back, I was always thankful that I had the breast every woman dreamed of, full, voluptuous breast that I could usually get away without a bra, and especially with this dress, a bra wasn't happening. The front was dipped low too, I always felt like one wrong move and a boob was going to flop out any second. It had very thin straps on the shoulders that always felt like they were going to break apart too. But I knew the material was well made and crafted. I never saw the price tag of the dress, but I knew Theo's taste and it was never cheap in any kind of way. I applied a little makeup and glanced over myself one last time in the mirror before sighing again "I suppose this will do." I said quietly to myself. I grabbed the black stiletto heels, they were open towed, with a strap across the top of my foot and a strap around my ankle. It snapped with a bow on the front, so it looked cute, and they were my favorite by far. As I walked out of my bedroom, I grabbed my little black clutch purse and grabbed a sparkly, almost see through shawl to wrap around my shoulders. I was about to walk out the door, when I heard a knock, and my phone rang at the same time. I stopped in my footsteps, confused as my phone continued to ring. I glanced down at my phone to see it was Theo, I quickly answered it "Hello...?" I answered, as another knock sounded on my door.

"Abby, I can't make it." I opened my mouth to reply, but he had already hung up. "Son of a bitch." I muttered to myself, as another knock sounded on the door "I'm coming!" I yelled, as I made my way to the door, I peeped through the peep hole and rolled my eyes as I unlocked the door and opened it to a scrawny kid holding a big bouquet of flowers "Miss Baker?" he asked, clearly struggling with the flowers "That's me." I said sheepishly. I let the guy inside and gestured towards the little island in the kitchen. I thanked the guy and closed the door behind him. Without even looking at the card, I knew immediately they were from Theo. I grabbed the card anyways and sure enough, it was Theo's way of apologizing for bailing tonight. I tossed the card into the trash and frowned at the flowers "As if this makes it any better." I said to them, glaring at them. "I broke up with you. We are done. Why don't you get that?" I talked to the flowers as if they were Theo, as if they could pass the message along. But I knew it was no use, Theo was set in his ways. He wasn't done. So, our relationship wouldn't be done until he said so. But damnit. I was done with him. I grabbed my phone and quickly sent a text *"Theo, we are done. I am serious. We are no more. I can't keep doing this. Find someone else."* I hit the sent button and sighed, I knew Theo wouldn't accept it, but he was going to have to.

I looked down at my outfit and frowned. I took all this time to get dressed up and for what? Nothing. I thought for a moment and decided to say screw it. I knew there was a gallery opening tonight, I was dressed the part, might as well go and enjoy it. I grabbed my stuff and headed out the door. Once outside, I hailed down a cab and headed off to the gallery opening. Once there, I paid for the cab and tipped him, I got out and made my way inside the gallery. It was for a new, upcoming artist. I wasn't fully sure who the artist was, but the paintings they did were amazing. They were portraits of beautiful women, men, couples, people with their children, dogs and even cats.

They did landscape paintings of various areas around New York City and what looked like maybe upstate New York, the countryside. I stopped at one in particular, a farm. I stood there for a moment, looking over every little detail. Then it clicked. I knew this farm. I grew up just up the road from it. I felt emotions wash over me as I studied it more. I felt an ache growing in my chest. My best friend lived there. I was at her house every night. Every summer breaks. Winter breaks. Holidays. Her family was my family. I began to feel tears well up in my eyes as the memories surged back to me. A dark memory flashed before my eyes, and I quickly made it disappear. I shook my head as I turned to move away from it, immediately bumped into what felt like a solid wall. I gasped as I almost fell backwards and was caught by strong arms. My eyes went wide at the man holding me.

"Nicholas." I said breathlessly. I stared up at him in amazement, as he stared down at me in what I could only describe as hunger. "Abigail." he said almost in a whisper. He slowly pulled me up into a straight standing position. I stood so close to him and then I wasn't. He pulled away quickly and a part of me felt offended by it, but I hid it. It was quiet between us for a moment before he motioned towards the painting of the farm "You like that one?" he asked. I glanced at it before looking at him and shrugged "It's okay, I suppose." I lied. It was amazing, but the ache I felt from seeing it hurt too much. It seemed he realized it caused me some kind of discomfort "I can remove it, if you don't like it. It's quite old anyways." he shrugged as he began to grab the painting. My eyes went wide, wondering what he was doing "Don't do that!" I pulled at his arm "I don't think the artist would like that." I told him, frowning. He gave me a grin that made my knees weak "I think he would understand." He pointed to the signature at the bottom of the painting. I read it. I looked at him, then back to the painting then back to him "You painted that? These?" I gestured around the gallery. He shrugged his shoulders as if it wasn't any big deal. I gaped at him, as I glanced around the gallery once more and was just shocked. His work was truly amazing. I looked back at him, and I felt a heat burn inside of me. It was as if I was the only person here. He didn't care for anything or anyone else around him "Your work is just truly amazing, Nicholas." I told him, with a soft smile. He smiled back at me, with a charming little smile that made my stomach do somersaults. We stood there, just staring at each other for what felt like an eternity before he broke eye contact with me and looked back at the farm painting. He began to remove it again, but I touched his arm and stopped him "Don't. It's beautiful. Just as I remember it." I said as I looked at the painting. I spent many hours inside that barn, playing around, chasing the chickens, helping with feeding the animals and cleaning stalls. I gently reached out to touch the painting, my fingers lightly touching the surface. I felt that ache to my chest again and let my hand drop to my side, as I felt his thumb brush away a tear that I didn't realize fell down my face. I looked up at him before looking away quickly, my face turning red as I sniffed "I've got to go." I said quickly as I walked as fast as I could in heels out the door. I felt the cool air hit my face instantly as I stepped outside. I took a deep breath in and let it out slowly. I started to hail a cab "Abigail!" I heard my name being called. I turned a bit and saw Nicholas come running out the door, he came to my side, and he looked like his new pet just died. It crushed me "I'm sorry..." I wasn't even sure what I was being sorry for. He half smiled, showing a dimple on his cheek "Don't be. I've had the painting removed. I can see it brings you pain." His smile went to a frown as he looked down at me, he had complete concern in his eyes and face for me "You shouldn't have done that. It was perfect. It was beautiful." I felt my throat get tight "I... It's okay." I pushed a smile to my lips "I'm just going to head home." I told him, when a cab finally pulled up. He opened the door for me, I could tell he was reluctant to let me leave, I didn't want to leave either "Are you sure?" he asked me, as I stood facing him, the cab door between us. No, I wasn't sure. I didn't want to leave, but the sane part of me was saying to go. "Yeah, I'm just going to go home. I shouldn't of came out.." especially after Theo being well, Theo. "Bye, Nicholas." I told him, as I slid into the cab seat in the back and reluctantly Nicholas closed the door. I stared at him for a moment through the window, faintly hearing the cab driver ask me where I wanted to go. I was torn. I bit the bottom of my lip before I rolled the window down "Do you want to go grab a coffee?" I asked him, hoping he would say yes, and by the way his face lit up at my question, I could tell he did. He nodded his head "Great. I just need to go change. I'll meet you there." He nodded in agreement, I asked if he knew of the little coffee shop in my neighborhood, I gave him the name, he said he did. I rolled the window back up and gave the cab driver my address. I felt my heart racing, I felt my soul soaring. But deep down, I also felt a sense of dread, foreboding. I didn't know why, so I just ignored it and shoved it away. As I got to my apartment, I paid the driver and went inside to immediately change and headed back outside to walk the couple blocks to the coffee shop. I couldn't stop smiling. I felt a happiness I hadn't felt in many years.

I arrived at the cute little coffee shop; I had spent tons of money here over the years since living in this neighborhood. It was a small business owned shop; the family could trace their lineage back to the first settlers coming to America in the 1700s. They had always been in the business of coffee and tea. They locally grew their own coffee and tea to brew at their shop. Everything in the shop, from the drinks to the food, was made from scratch and it was honestly the best around.

I stood there inside, smiling and greeting all the workers, they knew me by name there and they knew my order "Coming right up, Abby." the girl behind the counter said with a bright smile. I smiled back at her and nodded my head as I waited. I scrolled through my phone, checking my social media, replying to comments and messages and did the same for my business page too. I heard the bell above the door ring as the door opened, then heard a guy behind the counter yell "Nicholas! Hello!" That honestly shocked me as I turned to look at him in the doorway, with a sheepish grin on his face. He rubbed the back of his neck before waving to the man "Hey!" he replied as he made his way to me "How do they know you?" I asked him curiously, as the girl behind the counter brought me my coffee. I thanked her, giving her a tip and grabbed the cup. The other guy behind the counter, Rich, the owner of the coffee shop, chuckled at my question "Nicholas has been a long time...friend." I glanced at Nicholas who shrugged with a smile "Our families have known each other for years." he told him simply. "How come I have never bumped into you here before?" I asked him, I always hit this place up in the mornings before work and sometimes after work. And on my days off, I always go in and out of here. Nicholas shrugged again "Must have just come here at different times." I nodded my head; I suppose that would be true. He smiled down at me and grabbed his coffee from Rich, we took up a cute little table outside on the sidewalk. We sat across from each other, I sipped my coffee, as did he. Now that we were here, I had no idea what to do. What to say. But honestly, it wasn't awkward. It was, well, it was comfortable. It was like two friends that knew each other since birth, just having coffee together.

After a moment of silence, he cleared his throat "The gallery didn't seem like your first place to go earlier." he said it with a little grin to his lips. I felt my cheeks flush with heat, that dress had been so revealing. And all because Theo wanted me to wear it and he couldn't even show up for our date. I sighed, as I looked down at my coffee cup "I was supposed to go on a date. But the douchebag canceled it at the last minute." I shook my head before looking away from my cup and looking at him. The hatred in his eyes spoke volumes, he didn't even have to say a word. I felt it "But it's okay, though..." I said dismissively "I've told him before we were done, so I told him again when he canceled on me." I shrugged my shoulders "Hopefully the message is clear to him, and he doesn't act all high and mighty like no one can break up with Theodore Kingston." I chuckled at the thought of how Theo looked when he read my text message to him earlier. I could only imagine how he would react and wasn't surprised he didn't show up right away. But nonetheless, I was done with him. "Well, I hope he does get the message..." Nicholas told me, as he stared at me with hunger again, it made my insides burn. This man wanted to possess me, but not in the way that Theo did it. No, this was something different and I wanted it.

I cleared my throat and took a sip of my coffee, trying to shove the images and thoughts that popped into my head. I just met this guy. I didn't know him. But my soul screamed that I knew him, I felt so comfortable around him. I wanted to always smell his scent, to hear his voice, to see his smile, to hear his laughter. I wanted to be the one to make him smile and laugh. I wanted him more than the air in my lungs. And that was completely strange to me, I never felt a feeling like this. Even Theo didn't make me feel this way, not even when we first started dating. Was this what love at first sight was? Was this what it was to find your soul mate? I didn't know, but damnit if I didn't want to keep seeing this man every day for the rest of my life. I only hoped he felt the same way.

Nicholas felt like he was on fire. He felt a hunger inside of him that he never felt before in his life. He wanted Abigail, but not in a way that it seemed this Theo guy did. He wanted to make her smile, to see that light appear in her eye at things that brought her joy. To hear her laugh. He wanted to make Theo pay for any kind of pain he ever did towards Abigail. In all is years, he had never felt this way towards another woman. Except for one. But that was so long ago, a faint memory, but it still ached in his heart. But Abigail, she healed it, she made him feel like he could live again, but he knew he shouldn't even get close to her, to know her at all. It was wrong. In the end, it would just end in heartache again. But this time, of his own fault. It was why he stayed away from people. He kept to himself. He didn't get close to anyone and didn't let anyone get close to him. But Abigail, she was different. And he had a feeling he couldn't do anything to stop what was happening, he was falling for this beautiful woman that he stumbled upon one late night here at this very coffee shop. Apparently, she didn't remember, but he did. They bumped into each other as he was walking in and she was walking out, she had coffee in her hand, phone in the other hand to her ear and arguing with someone, he assumed it was probably Theo. The moment she touched him, he felt a shock go through him and he felt his body come alive. Her floral scent filled his senses, and he hasn't stopped smelling it since. So, when he found her store by accident too, he couldn't help but to pop in and just see her. He was hooked on her like a drug head hooked on drugs. But he did his best to stay distant, but life kept putting them in the same place and he was just going with it. Nicholas knew he should just leave and let it go, she was going to grow old, she would die, then he would be alone, once again. He felt an ache inside of him at the thought, should he just leave her and never know her, or deal with getting to know her, love her, have her and lose her? Which would hurt more? Honestly, right now, both felt like a knife to his heart even at the thought of them. Nicholas listened to Abigail as she talked, he smiled and nodded to her, though he was internally having a battle, he heard every word she said. He even replied to her when he needed to. He shoved the thoughts away when she mentioned about them taking a walk, he smiled at her, grabbed their cups and tossed them into the trash bin before returning to her. Nicholas held his arm out for her to wrap her arm around, the smile she gave him made his insides burn like fire, and her touch was gasoline to fuel it even more. God, he wanted her, he wanted her so badly, he could taste her.

I held his arm as we walked slowly, most of the time, not talking and sometimes just talking about random things, or something they saw interesting around the neighborhood they pointed out to each other. No one would ever know that the two of them had just met, they were completely comfortable together. I glanced up at him and smiled softly before I looked at where we had walked to. Apparently, we walked to my apartment without realizing it. My face flushed, as I stopped at the steps by the door "This is my apartment." I told him, I hesitated to ask him if he wanted to come inside, and before I could find the sane little voice to tell me don't do it, the words came out "Would you like to come inside?" I asked, he half smiled, looking like he was debating it as well, before he nodded his head "Yeah. That sounds good." I grabbed my key from my pocket, to unlock the main door into the apartments, I led him to the stairs, and we walked up to the top of the building, the fourth floor. I led him down a hallway to the corner apartment and unlocked the door and lead him inside. I was glad I wasn't a messy person. But when I didn't spend much of my time here, there was really no reason for it to ever get messy. I had no pets either, the apartment didn't allow them anyways. He shut the door behind us, I tossed my keys into a bowl on a stand near the door and sighed a bit, as I looked around, before my eyes landed on him. He just stood there by the door, he looked uncomfortable? Maybe, but I wasn't sure. I was starting to second guess asking him up here, maybe he didn't want to come up here and he was just being nice since I asked? I chewed the bottom of my lip and fiddled with the hem of my shirt as we stood there in silence for a moment *Well, say something, just don't stand there.* I thought to myself. "Umm, would you like something to drink?" I asked in a rushed voice. *Smooth, moron.* I mentally rolled my eyes at myself and smiled at Nicholas as he smiled back "Water is fine." he said, as I made my way to the kitchen "Make yourself comfortable." I told him, as I opened the fridge and grabbed two bottles of water. I closed the door to the fridge and made my way to the couch, where he was sitting, but he was sitting rigid. He sat on the edge of the seat like he was ready to spring into action at any minute. I handed him the water, I stood there and frowned "Are you okay?" I asked him, very concerned. Did I just put myself in danger by asking him up here? Was he getting ready to pounce on me and harm me? *Well, if he does, maybe I will like it..* I almost choked on the air I was breathing at my own thoughts, I cleared my throat, as he looked at me, raising one eyebrow "I'm okay." I said, clearing my throat again. Nicholas nodded "I'm fine too." he said, in a stern voice. I sighed, as I sat on the couch "If you want to leave, you can." I said, but it came out sounding disappointed, which, I was, but I didn't want him to know that. I saw out of the corner of his eye, he kind of slouched a bit and frowned "Oh.." he said quietly. I turned to look at him "Look, we were having a good time, and now it seems like you are awaiting to just leave at any second." I studied his face for a moment, he didn't look at me, and it seemed like forever before he did. He stared at me for a moment before he moved closer to me, I felt my heart race and pound hard against my chest. He got within inches of me. I felt myself leaning close to him, he leaned closer to me, my head swam with his scent swirling around me. I wanted him so much, I felt an ache inside of me. He got closer and I almost exploded at the thought of our lips touching, I began to close my eyes and then nothing. I blinked a few times, he was still so close to me. I bit my bottom lip as we sat there so close to each other. Just utter silence. He slowly reached up and brushed a few loose strands of hair from my face before he rested his hand against my cheek. His hand was calloused, rough, but yet soft and tender at the same time. Closing my eyes, I leaned my face into the palm of his hand, Nicholas closed his eyes, as he rested his forehead against mine. He sighed softly, before he slowly pulled away and dropped his hand down. I opened my eyes to stare into his and saw a sadness appear before it immediately disappeared. I opened my mouth to speak but instead his lips found mine. I melted to him, as I closed my eyes again and we kissed like we were long lost lovers, seeing each other for the first time in years. His arms wrapped around my waist, pulling my closer, my arms went around his neck, holding onto him as if my life depended on it. Our tongues danced together, I felt him growl against my mouth, as he gently pushed me down on the couch with him never letting go of me and our lips never leaving each other. I gasped when he trailed his lips from mine, across my jaw and down my neck. He placed tender kisses and nipped along the way. I bit my lip as I let out a soft moan. I felt him grin against my skin, a fire burned deep inside of me, I wanted him so badly and I could feel his excitement for me, growing against me. I wrapped my legs around his waist and pulled his hips closer to mine, he let out a gasp against my neck, as he pulled back some. He stared down at me with a hunger, a passion and fire inside of him, the same I felt and showed to him as I stared back up at him "Nicholas.." I said seductively. Next thing I knew, I was in his arms and he was carrying me to my bedroom.

Nicholas laid me gently down on the bed and began to undress me. He tossed my shirt off to the side and janked my jeans from me. He stood there staring down at me in just my bra and thong "You are the most beautiful woman I have ever met in all my years of being alive." I he softly. I felt my cheeks burn at his words, usually I didn't feel this comfortable with men, so exposed. But with Nicholas, I felt like a Goddess. I smiled up at him, as I reached up to tug at the hem of his shirt, he lifted it up over his head and tossed it off to the side. He never broke eye contact with me, as he undid his jeans and pulled them and his boxers down. I felt my heart pounding with excitement, as I looked at his swelled manhood. I trailed my eyes up his stomach to his face, as I burned with hunger for him. I could feel my thong getting moist with my excitement. Nicholas moved to be over top of me, he pressed himself against me and I moaned softly, as I lifted my hips up against him "Please." I was almost begging him. He chuckled, as he kissed my lips and made a trail from my lips, down to my stomach, I wiggled and squirmed against him, barely hanging on. His lips left a trail of fire, he kissed back up to my chest, he unclasps my bra from the back and tossed it off to the side. He stared in awe at my chest, as he took both hands and cupped my breast. His rough hands felt great against my smooth skin. He teased my nipples with his fingers, and I let out a moan as I arched my back. He bent his head down to take one in his mouth, his tongue dancing and teasing my nipple, he nibbled and sucked. He switched and did the same to the other. I gasped as I felt a hand trail down my stomach and slip inside of my thong to gently rub my clitoris. I moaned out, gripping the bed sheets, as I lifted my hips towards his hand. He slipped two fingers inside of me and I almost exploded with pleasure. He kissed his way down from my breast to my stomach. He removed my thong, and his mouth found my wetness and he began to tease and please me until I felt like I was going to melt into the bed. After only a moment, I gripped hard at the bed, and I let out a scream of ecstasy as I came. He kept going until I was spent. He kissed his way back up my stomach until he reached my lips. He kissed me gently, tenderly. He placed a hand against my face as we kissed slowly, passionately. I sighed contently, as he pressed his forehead against mine, then slowly he entered inside of me. I gasped at the feeling of him going inside of me. He began to thrust his hips slowly against mine, I moaned out softly as I moved mine against his. He went slow, both of us enjoying the pleasure it gave us. He buried his face in my neck, before letting out a low growl and rolling so that I was on top, and he was under me. I sat straight up, staring down at him, with my hands placed on his chest. I moved my hips slowly against him, biting down on my lip at the feel of him inside of me. He felt so amazing. I began to rock my hips faster; he grabbed my hips with his hands and rocked his hips against mine. I moaned out, as I was growing closer to my climax again. Our rhythm was in sync with each other, and I rode him faster and harder "Come for me, Abigail." he growled out, as he reached up and grabbed my breast, playing with my nipples. I gasped, as I moaned out in pleasure. Within a second, I came again, I cried out in the sheer pleasure of it, I felt like I was on cloud nine. And soon after, he let out a deep moan of pleasure and he came himself.

Immediately, I gasped as I jumped off of him and grabbed the sheet to cover myself "You didn't wear a condom!" I almost screamed at him. Though I was on birth control, there was always horror stories of women getting pregnant still. I began to panic "Oh, no. No. No." Nicholas looked confused, as he stood from the bed and tried to grab me to calm me down, I pulled away from him shaking my head "Why? Why would you do that?" I asked him, almost hysterically. "Abigail...Please. Just calm down." but I didn't feel calm, "I can't have kids." he told me. I completely froze. I stared at him in confusion "What?" I asked him, wondering if I heard him say "You can't? You're not just saying this?" Nicholas sighed, as he shook his head. A sadness came over him "I promise you; I cannot get you pregnant." That definitely calmed me down, but then I felt like a horrible person "I'm....I'm sorry." I didn't really know what to say. He shrugged his shoulders, as if it was no big deal. I moved closer to him, I reached out to touch his arm, I moved closer, I let the sheet fall down between us. He stared down at me, the sadness lingered, but it was slowly disappearing as that hunger in his eyes came over him. I slipped my arms up around his neck and softly kissed him. Nicholas wrapped his arms around my waist and kissed me back, he picked me up, my legs wrapping around his waist, as he led us back to the bed for another round.

4

The next morning, I woke up with the sun filtering in from through the curtains. I smiled, remembering the night before. I rolled over, but Nicholas wasn't there. I sighed, as I laid back down against my pillow and stared up at the ceiling. Should I be so surprised that he just up and left at some point? No. But I still was. I felt an ache begin inside of me, which then made me angry. I huffed as I crossed my arms over my chest "What's wrong?" I jumped a bit, as I heard his voice. I hugged the blanket to my chest, as I sat up in bed "Oh..I.." I felt my cheeks burn with embarrassment "I thought you left..." I told him. He smiled, as he chuckled and made his way to me. I realized that he was fully clothed. And he was in different clothes than last night "Actually, I did leave." he admitted as he sat down on the bed next to me "But, I only did to go home to change and grabbed some food and coffee." He said with a smile, as he leaned in and gave me a kiss. I leaned against him, kissing him back. God, I already wanted him again. And I lost count how many times I had him last night. Nicholas sighed, as he pulled away "Trust me, I want you too." he said, before he stood up "But, I unfortunately have plans I cannot miss today." I nodded my head "Okay. Umm, I guess I'll hop in the shower and get dressed really quick?" I left it a question hanging between us, hoping that he had time to wait around. He smiled and nodded "Fair enough. I'll be out here waiting." With that, he left the bedroom. I jumped from the bed and dashed to my bathroom to shower and dress quickly. I towel dried my hair and brushed it out before running my fingers through it quickly. I brushed my teeth and almost ran from the bathroom. I slowed myself down as I came out into the main area. He was standing there by the kitchen island, and smiled at me as he handed me my cup of coffee. I took a sip and sighed happily as he got my favorite "Thank you." He smiles with a nod, as he took a drink from his own. He had muffins, donuts, scones and bagels. He had sausage, eggs, bacon, and hash browns "I'll never be able to eat all this." I told him, as I began to add cream cheese to a bagel and take a bite "That's okay. I'll take whatever you don't eat and drop it off to a shelter." he said, "There is one not far from here and it's on my way." I nodded to him as I ate the bagel, then ate a donut and finished up my coffee. I helped him bag the rest of it up. I walked all the way down to the main doors of the apartment building. I stood outside on the curb with him as he hailed down a cab. I didn't want him to leave, but I knew he had plans he couldn't miss. Once the cab got there, he loaded the bags inside before turning towards me. He pulled me close to him, placing a hand on the side of my face, his fingers slipping through my hair and kissed me so passionately, I almost melted there on the sidewalk. I kissed him back, holding him close to me. When he pulled away, he was still very close to my face "I put my number into your phone. I'll text you when I can. I hope I can see you tonight." I smiled brightly "Yes." I told him, as he smiled back just as big as I was "Good. I'll see you then." He gave me one last kiss before he pulled away and got into the cab. I stood there watching him leave. I ached to be with him, I wanted to be with him. But instead, I sighed as I turned towards my apartment building and made my way back inside and up to my apartment. I closed the door behind me and locked it. I leaned against the door and stood there for a moment and realized I had never felt so happy in my entire life, especially with someone that I had just met for the very first time. I sighed contently, as I moved away from the door and went to grab a few things before I headed to my shop to get the store open for the day. I really needed to hire some people, but honestly, I just didn't want to go through the whole process and then there were trusting people with my business that I worked so hard to grow. Maybe one day. I left my apartment and hailed a cab. I got to my shop and went about the daily task of getting the store ready. I glanced at my watch and cursed under my breath. I was definitely behind today. I had people lined up at the door. I rushed to the door and unlocked it and flipped the sign from closed to open "Hi! Welcome! If you need any help, don't hesitate to ask! We still have the BOGO Free sale going on!" I let the customers know as I went back behind the counter and finished some things.

My day went by quickly. Before I knew it, it was after 2pm and once I had a moment to myself, I felt my stomach growl "Ugh.." I knew I needed to get some food, but the store got so busy, it was a mess. I sighed as I moved about the shop, picking things up, putting stuff back in their proper spots and tiding it all up. I was just about to deicide to close the store for lunch when I heard a customer come in "Sorry, I am closing!" I said, as I moved through the store to the front "Please come back.." I stopped in my tracks as I saw Theo. He didn't look happy. He looked pissed. "Abigail." he said, as he stood there, with his hands inside of his tailored dress pants. "Word on the street is you've got a new man." I felt my heart leap into my throat, but I stood there, crossing my arms over my chest, staring this man down "So what? We are not together anymore. I told you, Theo. We are done." He smirked, as he started to slowly walk around my store, he would stop and grab something breakable off a shelf, look at it and then just drop it to the ground, where it would shatter "Oops." he said in a smug ton "Hope it wasn't expensive." I glared at him, if looks could kill, he would be dead already "Theo. Please leave." He came around to me and pressed me up against a display case. He placed his hands on either side of my face and got close to me "You are mine, Abigail." he said in a threatening tone "I say when we are done. Not you. Me." he sneered "And I am not done with you, princess." he chuckled, and it sent chills down my spine "Here is what is going to happen. You either continue to be mine, or I'm going to destroy this shop, then I'm going to destroy your new boy toy." My eyes went huge, he wouldn't. He couldn't. I felt my breath catch in my throat, as I nodded my head. He grinned, giving me a kiss on the lips before pulling away and straightening himself up "Now, I have dinner party tonight with some big names, I need you there. I'll be at your place by 8pm sharp. Be ready." with that, he left the store, knocking over a few more breakable items on his way out. I was so beyond upset. I was angry, mad, frustrated, upset, hurt. I wanted to strangle the man. I quickly went to the door and locked it, turning the sign from open to close. I went to the back room and paced back and forth. I didn't know what to do. Though a part of me didn't want to believe Theo would be serious, another part of me knew he would. He would ruin my business. My life. Then he would go after Nicholas. Deep down, I knew it. I sighed, as I felt tears fall down my face. I wiped them away quickly. I grabbed my phone from my back pocket. I searched for Nicholas's number and found it. I opened a new text message and just stared at my phone. I felt more tears run down my face as I typed out the words. My heart broke into a thousand pieces.

I'm back with Theo. We should never see each other again. Sorry. Bye.

I hit send on the message. I stared at it for a second before I tossed my phone onto my desk. I sat down in the chair, placing my arms on my knees and burying my face in my hands. I bawled my eyes out for what seemed like forever. I kept hearing my phone ding with a message, one after another. I knew exactly who it was. But I couldn't bear to look at it. I put my phone on silent quickly, before I stood up, went to the bathroom and splashed water on my face. I stared at myself in the mirror. Just a few hours ago, I was the happiest woman alive. Now...Now I was miserable. I was broken. I took a deep breath and let it out slowly. I left the back room and went to the counter. I did my daily closing, even though it was only about 3pm. I closed early and went home. I quickly cleaned up the messes Theo made and made notes of the items he broke. After that, I made sure the store was locked up and left. I grabbed a cab and headed home. I made it up into my apartment, shutting the door behind me and locking it. I leaned back against it and slid down it, I pulled my knees to my chest and wrapped my arms around my legs, burying my face in my legs. I began to cry again; I heard the buzzing sound of someone ringing for my apartment number downstairs. I knew who it was. I didn't even have to look to call down to know who it was. I knew. *Nicholas.*

The buzzing stopped and I just sat there for a moment. I took a deep breath as I stood up, I needed a hot shower. I took two steps before there was a pounding at my door "Abigail! Please. Let me in! Talk to me!" I turned to stare at the door, "Go away!" I told him, "I don't want to see you." it was a big lie, I wanted to let him in. But I couldn't. Obviously, Theo had eyes everywhere, and I wasn't even surprised by that "Abigail, please. Just....Just let me in. Please." his voice was so broken, so sad. It made my heart ache so badly. I took a step towards the door before I stopped "I can't..." my voice cracked, as I tried not to cry again. He pounded on the door again "Abigail, please!" Nicholas was desperate. He knew there was no way she would go back to Theo. What they had...it was special. It was something he had never experienced in his entire life. Theo was no match for him, if the guy was threatening her or himself, he could handle him. He would protect Abigail, no matter what "Please open the door. Talk to me. If...If he is threatening you or me, I can handle it. I can deal with Theo." He spoke through the door, hoping so much she would just open it.

I stood there, staring at the door, wanting so much to open it. To see him, to be held in his arms. To feel secure and safe. Before I could stop myself, I unlocked the door and opened it, Nicholas pulled me into his arms so quickly, I got dizzy, but I clung to him, I closed my eyes and buried my face into his chest as I sobbed "He will kill you, Nicholas." I choked out, as I looked up at him "He will destroy my business." Nicholas placed his hands on either side of my face and stared down at me "I promise you, Abigail, I won't let that man harm you, or your business." he gently kissed my forehead and pulled me into a hug again, holding me close to him. I sighed, wanting to believe that he could protect me, but deep down, I always knew Theo was something else. He always had that *I'm the big bad wolf* type of vibe. Was he the mob? I didn't know, but it was something scary, especially after earlier. He warned me, and here I stood in the arms of the man

Theo threatened to kill if I ever saw him again. I pulled away from Nicholas, my eyes wide with terror as I looked up at him, tears swam in my eyes "You need to leave. Theo will know you are here. I don't know how, but he will." I trembled, wrapping my arms around myself "Please." Nicholas stood his ground, he wasn't leaving her alone, if Theo wanted a fight, he would give him one. And the man would regret it deeply "No. I'm not leaving you." I frowned at him and shook my head "He's picking me up for a date, if I don't show, he will definitely know." I felt the tears fall down my face, Nicholas cringed at seeing the tears. He sighed, as he gently grabbed me and pulled me over to the couch. He sat me down and sat down beside me. I rubbed my eyes and face with the sleeve of my shirt, I sniffed some and let out a tired sigh. This day had been so exhausting. Nicholas stared at me, just letting me have the moment of quiet, I needed it. I had to think. But my brain didn't want to work. My heart was telling me to just say screw Theo and just stay right here with Nicholas. I fiddled with the bottom of my shirt, staring at it like it held all the answers I needed. I chewed the bottom of my lip, trying to figure this all out. There was only one thing I could do. I looked up at Nicholas, no emotion on my face "Please, just leave." he shook his head "Nicholas. Go. I don't want you." I stood up and crossed my arms over my chest, giving him a hard look "Get out. Now." Nicholas stood up, a look of confusion crossed his face, I felt my heart ache, but I kept the hard look to face and showed no other emotion, he had to believe that I really didn't want him. How else could I protect him? "Get. The. Fuck. Out." I started to move towards the door, but he grabbed me quickly, pulling me close to him. I stared up at him, as he stared down at me, my heart raced with how close were together, but I did my best to keep the emotion off my face "Your heart gives you away." he said quietly. I furrowed my brows, in confusion, there was no way he could hear my heart pounding so hard in my chest. I quickly shook my head and wiggled my way out of his arms "No, it doesn't. Just get out. Right now, I don't want you. I'm back with Theo and that's that." I told him. Nicholas was very confused but sighed as he turned to head out the door. He felt defeated. He wanted her, he knew she wanted him too. What was she doing? Trying to protect me? He got the door and opened it, he turned to face her before he left "Abigail. Please. I can protect you. I can keep you safe." I walked towards the door and kept the cold hard look to my face "I don't need you." I slammed the door shut and locked it. I placed my hand over my mouth as I stepped back away from the door and wrapped my other arm around my stomach *God, even I hate myself.* I thought, as I felt the tears stream down my face. I let my hand fall down from my face, I turned to go towards the window that faced the street and peered out the curtain. I watched as Nicholas exited the building and stepped onto the sidewalk. He glanced back towards the building, where I quickly hid from his viewing, hoping he didn't see me looking. I peered again and he was gone. I sighed, as I stepped away from the window and stood there for a moment. I let out a scream, as my gut felt like it had just got punched. I hated Theo so much. Why would he do this? Why did I have to think I was in love with that man so many years ago? Honestly, I think I only pretended to be because of his money. He gave me the things and dreams I wanted. And when I didn't need him for that anymore, I didn't feel love towards that man. I felt the anger boil in my blood, one way or another, Theo was going to let his hold go of me. Even if I had to figure out a way to kill the man.

Over the next few days, I slipped into a persona of being the woman that Theo wanted. Submissive Abigail. I did what he said without complaint. Which gave me some perks too. I talked Theo into hiring a few people to run my shop for me, people that could be trusted and would take care of it. If I was planning on getting rid of Theo, I would have to be free of all distraction and the shop was definitely a big one. I thought about different ways to try to be rid of Theo. One was finding him someone else, another woman. But, when I tried one night, it led to us having a threesome and then he angrily told the woman to get out and tossed her clothes out the window. I had felt so bad for the woman, but I had kept my face stone cold and just shrugged my shoulders to her. I wasn't sure why he got angry, maybe because I found myself enjoying the woman pleasuring me more than I did Theo when he did it? It wasn't my fault, he only cared about pleasing himself and no one else. It resulted in him having rough angry sex, but surprise to him, I enjoyed it rough, so it became a win for me. He didn't like it so much that I enjoyed that kind of sex more than what he usually did, which you could say was vanilla. Which resulted in him trying a few different things that he didn't think I would enjoy; I did my best to *act* like I didn't enjoy it, but it was definitely hard to do. I sighed as I laid there on Theo's bed, staring up at the ceiling, he was in the bathroom cleaning himself up. My hands were still bound to the bed post on either side of my head. I wiggled to get into a somewhat upright position, and frowned as I looked around. Hopefully he wouldn't forget to untie me. I looked towards the bathroom door as it opened and walked out, still completely naked, but smelling fresh from his shower. He had a smirk on his face as he sauntered his way towards me. I raised an eyebrow at him as he reached the bed and picked up the whip laying on the bed. He gently tapped it against my thigh before smacking it down on my thigh. I hissed, as I bit my lip and gripped my hands into fist. He chuckled, as he did it again. I noticed him getting hard again, causing a little grin to come to my lips. I wiggled a bit on the bed, adjusting myself, causing my breast to jiggle, Theo stared at them as if they held the answers to the world. I smirked, as I made them jiggle some more "You like them?" I asked him seductively. Theo licked his lips, as he climbed onto the bed, positioned himself between my legs and spread them as far as they would go. I gripped at the ropes that tied me to the bed "I sure do." he said in a deep tone, almost growling it out. It caused chills to run down my spine. A part of me felt like maybe I created a monster when he realized that I liked the rough, kinky sex. But another part of me was really enjoying it and liking this new side of Theo. He began to tease me in various ways. Making me squirm and wiggle against his touch, wanting more and more. He reached into a drawer on his bedside table, grabbed a toy and pulled it out. He grinned as he showed me vibrating butt plug. It tapered at the very end, but it grew wider and wider as it got to the studded end. He untied on hand and motioned for me to roll over. I bit my lip, as I rolled over, he grabbed my hips, putting me on my knees and pulling my ass up into the air. He squirted some lube on my butt hole, and then onto the butt plug as well. Theo gently inserted the plug, first going slow and gently, I gasped loudly, moaning out as he began to pick up speed by thrusting it, but he was still gentle. He eventually inserted the entire plug inside of me, he turned on the vibrating part of it, causing sensual pulses to run through me. He reached around to rub my clitoris, causing more pleasure to ripple through me. I felt like I was going to explode into a thousand pieces. I moaned loudly "Oh, Theo!" I said, biting my lip. I heard him chuckle behind me, as he positioned himself on my back, his very hard manhood rubbing against me, as he moved my hair from neck, he began to kiss and nibble, causing me to be turned on more. He pulled back, holding onto my hips, as he slipped himself inside of me, I was so wet, Theo let out a moan as soon as he entered me. I gasped as he thrusted hard against me, slapping my ass as hard as he could, I knew I would have a handprint there for a while, but Theo loved that. He slapped it hard again, as he thrusted as hard as he could against me. He reached up, grabbing hold of my neck, and began to squeeze. I moaned out, as I closed my eyes, enjoying the pleasure that this man was giving me. He let go of my neck, of my neck, untying my other hand as he pulled out of me and moved off the bed. He stood there by the edge and motioned for me to come to him. He grabbed his cock and slowly began to stroke it "Suck it." he told me, I nodded my head as I moved into position to give him a blowjob. He grabbed a fist full of hair and fucked my mouth. He moaned as I sucked hard and licked all over. He gripped hard my hair and pulled my mouth back as he stroked himself with the other and let out a loud groan as he came. I opened my mouth as he spewed his seed all over my mouth and face. Once he was done, I licked my lips, as I opened my eyes and stared up at him. He tossed me a towel from the bedside table, I wiped off my face and mouth and tossed the towel to the floor. I still had the butt plug inside of me, vibrating away, the slightest movement sent a jolt of pleasure through me. I moaned out at every little movement. Theo chuckled, as he reached into the bedside table and pulled out a little remote. He hit a button the vibrating stopped. I raised an eyebrow at him "Well, that's a neat toy." he nodded his head, as he looked down at the remote and hit a button again to turn it back on, he upped the intensity of the vibrating and I moaned out, squirming on the bed. Theo seemed to enjoy that. He hit the button again and turned it off. I sighed out, breathing a little heavily "You'll be joining me today. And this." he held up the remote "Will be my way of keeping things interesting today." he smirked as he watched as my eyes went wide and my mouth dropped open "What?" I said, wondering if I had heard him correctly. Theo just walked away, going to the bathroom again, as he did he turned on the vibrating butt plug and I groaned as pleasure ran through me. After a few moments, he came out cleaned up again and turned it off again. I laid there panting, I had come so close to coming and he stopped it. I sighed, as my hand went down to my side. "Go get cleaned up." he ordered me as he began to dress himself. I nodded as I went to the bathroom and hopped into the shower real quick. When it seemed I was taking to long, he turned the toy on and I almost fell to my knees, I let out a loud moan "Hurry up!" he yelled, as it turned off again. I cursed him under my breath as I quickly finished. I got out, dried off and walked out to the bedroom to see dress laid out for me. There was no bra or underwear "Um, where is my bra? Underwear?" I asked him, as I stood there, a hand on my hip, glaring at him. He held the remote up, ready to push the button and I sighed "Fine!" I said, as I grabbed the very thing black dress and slipped it on. Of course, it was flawless, it felt amazing against my skin and when the fabric rubbed against my already hard, sensitive nipples, I let out a gasp, as I bit my lip. Theo chuckled, as he moved closer to me. He flicked on of my hard nipples, causing me to moan slightly. He ran his hand up my thigh, raising the dress up and pressed his fingers against my clitoris, and running them down me, I was soaked already he was enjoying this far to much "Mmm, good." he said, as he pulled his fingers away and sucked my juices off them. He growled at the taste "Ready?" he asked, as he held his arm out for me to hold, I sighed and nodded. We walked through the house and out the door into his personal car with driver. I wasn't sure where we were going, I didn't really pay much attention. I didn't really care either. My plan seemed to have went sideways. I was suppose to be getting rid of Theo, not this. He found my kink and now he was enjoying it way to much. And if I admitted to myself, so was I. *Damnit.* After a while, we arrived to where ever. Another mansion of someone rich that Theo knew. I climbed out the car and followed Theo around like a good little puppy. I smiled, I acted the part of a loving significant other. I shook hands, I received way to many looks from way to old guys that looked like they wanted alone time with me and it made me wanted to puke. The sad thing was, she was sure if they offered the right amount, Theo would let it happen too. I made sure I stuck to him until I knew I would be safe away from the old perverts. And lucky enough, Theo made it clear he wasn't sharing me with anyone tonight and that anyone so much as land a hand on me, he would gut them. It was reassuring enough for me to be able to wander around, especially since Theo said he had "business" to discuss with some of those perverted men in another room and I couldn't be there. Theo made sure I didn't wander very far either. He knew how far the remote worked and he made sure I didn't wander any further than it could go.

I stood almost in a corner by myself, I stood there, looking around at all these people. All of them were rich in one way or another. Whether it was through old money or dirty new money. And it was usually made in a way that wasn't good either. I made my way to the table where a guy was setting up more glasses of champagne and wine. I smiled as I grabbed a cup of red wine. I took a sip as I walked around the room. I faintly listened to what the people were saying, it wasn't anything good or interesting. They all talked about the same thing: who was stealing their money, who was fucking their partner and who's partner they was fucking. I rolled my eyes as I found a pair of doors that opened to a balcony. I made my way outside onto the balcony and the sound of the people became very faint. I took a deep breath as I closed my eyes and felt the cool air brush against my face. I sighed as I opened my eyes and stared out into the darkness. What I wouldn't give to just run away right now. My plan was going to shit. And I knew it. Theo had me in his clutches and he wasn't going to let go. I downed the rest of my wine and set the cup down on the little table. I took another deep breath in, smelling the scents of the countryside. It made my heart skip a beat as a face flashed across my mind. I felt my breath catch and tears well up into my eyes. Why did I do it? Why did I shove him away? I cursed myself, as I grabbed the balcony rail and gripped hard and at the exact moment, Theo hit the button on the butt plug and a rush of pleasure swept through me. I bit my lip from moaning out loudly. I felt like I was going to explode when it finally stopped. I gasped, realizing now I was holding my breath. I panted, as I leaned over the rail, trying to catch my breath. Damn him. Damn him to hell. I stood up right, and turned to leave the balcony, but instead I hit a solid wall. I let out a yelp, as arms caught me from falling backwards. The man held me tight, but gently. I looked at the face of the man and I thought I was dreaming "No.." I said quietly as Nicholas stared down at me with surprise and confusion "Abigail." he said in a whisper, almost not believing it himself. He slowly raised me up to an upright position and took a step away from me "Nicholas..Wha...What are you doing here?" I asked, as I frantically looked around, hoping no one saw. I grabbed his arm to move him away from the doorway of the balcony so no one could see either of them. "I was going to ask you the same thing." he said, realizing what I was doing. "Well, I am here with Theo. He had business to tend to." I told him, like it should have been so obvious. He nodded his head. I sighed, as I looked away from him. I wanted to tell him I was sorry, to take back every word I ever said to him. I even began to open my mouth to say so, until I felt that pulsing vibration going through me. I almost doubled over from it and bit my lip hard, causing it to bleed. I hissed as I tasted the blood "Damnit!" I touched my lip, seeing the blood on my fingers. The vibrating stopped almost as quickly as it began, and I mentally was cussing Theo out a thousand times over. I looked at Nicholas and the look upon his face made me step back a few steps away from him, I had never seen him look like that. It was like he was a predator, ready to pounce on its prey. He had a hunger to his eyes that was different from the sexual hunger I had seen before. "Nicholas.." the words came out softly, quietly. I was almost afraid to speak. He just stared at my lip, as the blood dripped down my chin to my neck. I didn't move, as he stepped towards me, never taking his eyes off the blood. I stood frozen. He reached up to wipe the blood from my lip with his thumb, then licked it from his thumb. He closed his eyes, as he groaned. Whe he opened his eyes, they weren't the bright darkness they usually were, instead they were just dark. Deadly. "Abigail.." he said through gritted teeth. I felt my heart pound heavily through my chest "Run." he told me. It didn't register in me what he said, I stood there, still frozen, like a deer caught in headlights "Wha--" I didn't even get the words out before he pulled me to him, he turned to press me against wall, grabbing my wrist and pressing them against the brick wall above my head. I gasped, not sure what the hell was happening here. He put his face very close to mine, before licking at my lip where I bit it and then trailing down to my chin and neck, lapping up the blood as if he was a dog dying of thirst. I felt a chill run through me, I wasn't sure if it was fear, pleasure or both. I tried to loosen my wrist from his grip, but Nicholas held tight. He let out a growl, as he sniffed at my neck, my pulse was pounding, my heart was racing "Nicholas..Please." I said, the fear showing in my voice, I had no idea what was happening, but I did know that if Theo found us like this, we would both be dead for sure. "Nicholas." I begged. He looked at me, blinking a few times, before he shook his head. He slowly let go of his grip around my wrist and let my arms drop to my side. I rubbed at my wrist as I looked up at him confused "I..I'm sorry." he said, before turning from me and disappearing back into the house. I went to search for him, but as I stepped inside, Theo found me "There you are." he said with a grin. I tried to casually find Nicholas without making it look like I was looking for someone "Here I am." I told him, with a sweet smile. Theo pulled me close to him, I could feel the bugle of him hard against me, he grinned down at me "I'm going to fuck you so hard." he whispered to me, as he kissed my neck. I shivered as he began to pull me from the room, we made our way throughout the house until we found a room. He opened the door and checked to make sure no one was in there. I followed me inside, he grabbed me, picking me up, I wrapped my legs around him, as he kissed me hard and feverishly. He growled against my lips, as he sat me down on the huge mahogany desk. He raised my dress up more, as he undid his pants quickly, he let them drop to the floor. He grabbed the remote from his jacket, before tossing it off and to the side. He pushed the button on the remote, at the same time he thrust hard inside of me. I let out a scream of pleasure. I arched my back, as he thrust hard against me, Theo pulled the top of my dress down to reveal my breast, he grabbed them in his hands, squeezing them, he dipped a head down to suck on one, lick and bite and then went to the other. I ran my fingers through his hair, as I gripped a handful. He growled against my chest, as he lifted his head up "You are mine." he growled out, as he stared at me. I moaned out, nodding my head "I'm yours." I moaned out. Theo wrapped his arms around me, lifting me up off the desk, we moved to the couch, where he sat down. I rode him hard and fast. I was close to coming, I was ready to explode when I felt Theo let out a moan, he gripped my hips hard, moving me harder and faster against him "Theo!" I cried out, as I felt my own climax come, I rode him until we were both spent. I sighed as I sat there, my face buried into his neck. I kissed his neck gently, rubbing my hand up and down his chest. Theo sighed contently, as he wrapped his arms around me. He reached down my back to the butt plug and gently pulled it out. I gasped as he did so, he tossed it onto the couch next to us. I felt a sort of relief having it gone, but having it there for so long, it felt odd that it was gone. Theo lifted my face up to his, he gently kissed me before he pulled back. He gripped my chin hard so I couldn't move and keep eye contact on him "I can smell another man on you." his voice was in a normal tone, but his eyes were burning daggers at me "What? I..I was with no one." I told him. How..How could he know? He smirked as he let go of me and shoved me off of him onto the couch. I sat there for a moment before adjusting the dress on me. He dressed himself and made himself look all neat and clean again "Don't like to me, Abby." he said, straightening out his cuffs, as he stared down at me. I stood up and crossed my arms over my chest "Theo. I wasn't with anyone. I'm here with you. Only you. I went to the balcony for some air. It's stuffy in here." I told him. It really wasn't a lie. Did he see Nicholas leave the balcony I was on? God, I hoped not. I moved towards him, I placed my hand on his chest "Theo. I'm yours." I stared up at him, with seductive eyes, as I trailed my hand down to the crotch of his pants and gently began to rub. I felt him start to harden again "Only yours." I told him, as I leaned up to kiss at his neck "Yours forever." I whispered, as I nipped at his ear. I felt him shudder and let out small groan, as I continued to rub against him "I only want you." He finally loosened up a bit and relax, but he grabbed at my hand rubbing him and stopped me "It will have to wait til we get home." he said disappointingly. He turned off the butt plug and placed it into his pocket. He grabbed my hand and walked from the room. We both went back to the part of people for another hour or so, I lost track. I just knew I was ready to leave. When we finally did, I was more than happy to almost run out the door. I kept begging Theo to leave, rubbing on him, bending over in front of him to either give him a great view of my ass or my cleavage. I was happy when it finally worked, especially since some of the old perverts were getting a little to handsy with me. When we got back to Theo's house, he practically dragged me to his bedroom, tore the dress off of me and before I could even say a word, he was on top of me. We went on for hours before Theo finally fell asleep and I laid there, naked in his bed, staring up at the ceiling with one thought on my mind *Is Nicholas a vampire?*

5

⊙⟨⟨⟩⟩

Over the next few days, I was alone at Theo's, minus all his workers, Theo himself was gone. He had "business" he said he had to attend to in Chicago. I pretended to be sad about him leaving, saying how much I was going to miss him. Eventually, he left, and the workers didn't really pay much attention to me. They did their jobs and I stayed out of their way, I mainly stayed in Theo's bedroom. I only left when I wanted to stretch my legs or got hungry. I sat there at his desk, on my laptop and did research. I couldn't stop thinking about Nicholas. The way he reacted to my blood. How he became feral. And I swear on my life, before he let go of me, I thought I saw fangs! But it was impossible, right? I kept telling myself I was going crazy. That entire day/night was just crazy. Maybe I wasn't in my right mind because of Theo and then running into Nicholas. Maybe Nicholas just had a fetish for blood? I cringed at the thought and rubbed my neck. I searched the internet for hours about vampires, the lore behind them, were they real, could they be real. Is it even possible!

After a couple hours of searching, I sighed, as I scrolled through a page. I sat up straight and stretched, I yawned. I really needed to take a break. As I started to close out the page, I stopped when something caught my eye *Roanoke*. Living in one of the original 13 colonies, we learned about Roanoke Colony, or The Lost Colony as it was known. I sat there, reading through the article. It was a theory about what happened to the almost 120 colonists. *Vampires.* My eyes went wide. I scooted to the edge of my chair, reading more. The article stated that there was evidence found, but it had been quickly tossed away, that vampires were the reason behind them all disappearing. The vampires had already been here in the states before settlers began to come. Apparently, the settlers had been warned, told them to stay away from the area they wanted to settle in. But they didn't listen. Theory is that a rouge vampire attacked them all. The vampire had been banished to the area, cursed to never feed on another human again. But when the settlers came, one by one, they all began to disappear. It was slow at first, but eventually, the vampire got greedy, he started making new vampires and they needed to feed too. I closed the laptop and sat there in utter shock. Would it be possible? Was Nicholas a vampire? Maybe even one from The Lost Colony? I shook my head as I stood up. I had to find an answer. I had to figure this out. I paced the room for a moment, before I grabbed my cell phone. I tried to call Theo, but he ignored it. I rolled my eyes and groaned. I clicked on messages and clicked his name;

Theo, I need to run into the city. I want to check my shop to make sure everything is going smoothly. I also want to stop by my apartment to grab a few things and do some shopping. Are you fine with this?

I sent the message. I watched as the three little dots appeared meaning he was texting back. He replied with a simple *Yes.* That was easy enough, I guess. I grabbed my jacket and purse; I slipped on my shoes and practically ran downstairs. I went outside and glanced around "Hey!" I yelled to the driver "I need a ride into the city. To my shop." the man nodded, as he walked to a car and opened a door for me. We couldn't get to the city quick enough. I hopped out of the car at my store. The driver began to get out himself, I stopped him "Don't worry. I will call you when I am ready for a ride back. I don't know how long I will be. I have other things to do." he didn't really like my answer "Theo said it was fine." I showed him our messages and the guy nodded his head, as he merged into traffic and left. I stood there for a moment, I peeked into the store, it looked fine. I hailed a cab and gave my address. I paid the cab driver as we came to a stop at my apartment. I got out and stood there on the sidewalk for a moment. I watched all the people walking around, up and down both sides of the streets. Was it possible any of these people were vampires? But with all the lore I found, they couldn't be in the daylight. I sighed, as I made my way down to the coffee shop. I hoped like hell that Nicholas was there. When I walked inside, I glanced about and didn't see him. The girl behind the counter saw me and smiled "Hey, Abby! The usual?" I shook my head "No, actually, I'm looking for Nicholas.." I said, hoping maybe she could help me. She got ready to open her mouth when Rich stepped up to the counter "He isn't here." I frowned, obviously he wasn't "Well, yeah. I can see that." I said, "Do you know where I could find him?" I asked, Rich looked like he didn't want to tell me, which meant he did know "Come on, I have to find him, I need to speak to him." I begged. "He just left!" said the girl, who realized she probably shouldn't of said it, from the look on Rich's face "He went that way." she pointed left out the door. I smiled happily at her "How long ago?" I asked her, "About a minute ago. Right before you came in!" I was almost running out the door as she spoke those words. I went left out the door, searching through all the people and glancing into all the stores as I went by. I hoped I could find him, I had to know. I had to get answers. When I finally felt like I would never find him, I heard it. His voice. I would know it anywhere. I stopped, I heard his laugh and my heart leaped from my chest as I turned, ready to yell his name, but then stopped. My heart sank, as I saw him sitting at a little bistro table in front of a café with a beautiful blonde woman. I just stood there, people having to walk around me as I stared at them. Nicholas was laughing at whatever the woman said, he reached to touch her hand, when his eyes found me. He immediately froze. The woman turned to look at me, before looking back at him "Nicholas.." she said, with almost the same accent as him, I blinked a few times before shaking my head "I'm..I'm sorry." I said before turning to leave. It shouldn't hurt, but it did to see him with someone else. But I did tell him to go. I told him I didn't want him. I wanted Theo. I kept walking, not even sure where I was going.

I turned a corner and kept going. I slowed down and glanced

around. It was an alley, but it ended. I sighed, as I turned to go back and stopped in my tracks. I let out a yelp "Nicholas!" I placed a hand over my heart, as he had almost scared me to death "Sorry.." he said, "I called out to you, but you must of not heard me." he said, I felt my cheeks burn at that, I really didn't hear him call out to me. I was so lost in my thoughts; I didn't even notice where I had walked to either. I had so many questions for him, but all I could think of was the woman he had been with. And now all I had was questions about her, even though it was really none of my business "Look, Lucy is just a friend. I've known her since I was baby. She was in town, so we were having lunch together." he explained himself, as if he was caught cheating. Which, it kind of felt like it, but I knew that was not what it was "Nicholas, you don't have to explain yourself to me." I told him "You owe me nothing..." he really didn't, but he looked as if he did. I sighed, as I looked around at where we were before looking back at him "Can we go somewhere to talk?" I asked him, I had to get answers before I convinced myself that I was insane. "Sure. Umm..My place is just up the block?" he offered, I nodded my head "Sure, that sounds good." I followed him up the block to his place. It was a brand-new building in the area. It was all metal, glass and modern. I made a face at it, he chuckled, "Don't like it?" I scoffed as I looked at him "It looks cold. Dead." when I realized what I said, my face went blank, and I felt stupid. I cleared my throat and looked away "I mean, it's just so modern..." I mumbled. Nicholas agreed as he led me inside the building and up to the very top floor. The apartment was pure natural light. Windows everywhere. Sky lights all across the ceiling. I was honestly in awe of it. I did love natural light. It was the best. "Make yourself comfortable." he gestured towards the living room, I made my way slowly over to the living room, looking at everything as I passed it. He had a ton of paintings, she assumed ones he did himself. He had relics from the past, things that looked like they belonged in a museum. They were magnificent.

I sat on the couch, as Nicholas joined me with a couple cups of ice water, I smiled as I grabbed a cup and took a sip. I sat the cup down as

I turned to look towards him as he sat down next to me. I really wasn't sure how to go about even asking this. Did I come right out and just say it. Or did I talk about something randomly and slowly bring it up? I struggled with finding the right way. Nicholas reached out to grab my hands, I apparently was fiddling with the bottom of my shirt and didn't realize it. "Abigail. What is it?" he asked me, as I looked away from our hands and back to him. *Okay, Abby. Just say it. Just ask him. You can do it. Say it.* "Are you.." I choked on the words, I couldn't get them out "Am I what?" he asked curiously "Are you doing okay?" I forced the words out and internally hated myself. *Moron.* I agreed with myself. He looked at me as if he knew that was not what I wanted to say, but he smiled, as he brought my hand up to his lips and gave my knuckles a gently kiss "I am perfect." he said, I almost melted right there on the couch. "But is that really what you wanted to ask me?" he questioned as he let my hand go gently, he reached up to brush some hair from my face. Honestly, being this close and him touching me, I couldn't even think straight "Uhh, what?" I said, laughed, as I shook my head. I sighed as I stood up and paced a bit "Sorry.." I didn't know what to do. I stopped by a window and stared down at the people below. I closed my eyes, trying to center myself, but then I felt him next to me. I opened my eyes and turned to see him standing next to me. I stared up at him "Just ask me, Abigail." it was like he knew what I already wanted to say, but the words wouldn't come out "Abigail. Ask me." he said the words a little more fierce, his face got hard. It made me take a step back "Do it." he said, raising his voice a bit, I shook my head, as I took another step back, Nicholas took a step towards me, I took another step back and felt a wall. I felt my flight or fight kick in, as Nicholas stood close to me, he placed a hand on the wall above my head and leaned down "Just ask me." he said, quietly. I stared up at him, I opened my mouth to speak, but nothing came out "Do it!" I jumped at his loud words and then I heard someone speak, not realizing it was me "Are you a vampire!" I rushed the words out, I clapped my hands over my mouth, as he leaned back away from me. He took a step back as he just stared down at me. It was quiet between us as the words just hung there. Nicholas stared at me then he began to laugh, I big belly laugh, like he had never laughed so hard in his life. I frowned, placing my hands on my hips, glaring at him. I didn't see how this was *that* funny. Nicholas settled himself down, wiping away a tear "I'm sorry, Abigial. Really." he said, smiling at me. I still wasn't smiling, I was glaring daggers at him "This isn't funny." I told him, as I huffed and crossed my arms over my chest. He smiled and chuckled as he moved closer to me, placing his hands on my arms and unfolding my arms from my chest to grab my hands. He brought them up to his lips and kissed them both, before lowering them but still holding my hands "Yes." he said simply. At first, I kind of forgot what he was saying yes to. I smiled, then it disappeared as I realized what I had asked him. I went to move away, but he kept a hold of me, I felt the flight or fight kick in again and it was telling me to run. He had been so serious when he said yes. "Are..Are you messing with me?" he still stayed serious, as he shook his head "No." I kept trying to get out of his grip "Abigail. Stop. Please." I stopped moving, as I stood there staring up at him "I can explain." he let go of one hand and motioned towards the couch, he led me there, still holding one hand, as if he was afraid, I was going to take a run for it. Which, my body was telling me to do just that. We sat on the couch, he took a deep breath before he spoke "I've been alive for far too long, Abigail. I've seen everything that you could possibly see. I've watched people come and go. I've been there for every new stage this country went through." It was hard hearing this. He looked away from me as if looking at something far away, maybe in the past. "I came here in the late 1500s. I was with the settlers of Roanoke. The Lost Colony. There were over 100 of us, thriving. We had some hard times, but we eventually made it. We were surviving." He smiled at the memory as he spoke "I was to be wed. To the most beautiful woman I had ever seen." He looked back at me with such a sad expression that it broke my heart. He shook his head "Anyways, there was this rouge vampire. He was banned to the area we settled in. Every so often people would go missing. We assumed it was the Indians, they had warned us to not settle there, we thought maybe it was their land. We were so wrong. Eventually people became to disappear and then come back…But it wasn't them." he said the last part quietly, as he got lost in the memory "They were hungry. So hungry. But food didn't satisfy them. What they wanted, what they needed was blood." he looked at me, I just sat there frozen, listening to him tell me all of this. Did I really believe it? "It was late one evening, I was searching for my wife to be, people told me to give up. To not wander so far away from the settlement. But I did. I had to find her. I had to see if she was okay…" he looked down at our hands, he gently rubbed my knuckles, "I did find her." he glanced up at me, choking on his words "What was left of her." he sucked in a breath and let it out slowly "They tore her to pieces." he said quietly. I felt my throat tighten, I felt tears sting my eyes. I threw my arms around his neck and hugged him close to me, I felt the tears slide down my face. For a moment, Nicholas didn't know what to do, until he felt me sobbing. He hugged me tight, not wanting to let go. I buried my face in his neck "I'm so sorry, Nicholas.." I said softly. He pulled away enough to look at me. He smiled down at me, brushing away the tears with his thumb "It's okay, Abigail. It was so long ago. It still hurts, but I've moved on. I've healed." he promised her, as he cupped her face. I stared up at him, as he smiled down at me, I could see the sadness in his eyes, but I could see that he truly meant it, he was sad about it, who wouldn't be, but it was a memory, it was gone and done "Did you ever find out who the rouge vampire was?" I asked him. He sighed, as he let his hand drop from my face and shook his head "No." I frowned thinking for a moment "Do you think he is still out there somewhere?" I asked. Nicholas nodded his head "I believe he is. I never really saw who he or she was. So I have no idea what they looked like. They could have been anyone." he said shrugging his shoulders. I nodded my head "So, Lucy was a part of your settlement group?" I asked curiously. Nicholas smiled down at me "Yes. Our parents built their homes next to each other. They always thought we would get married, but Lucy..Well, she likes women. Not men." he laughed, shaking his head "If her parents EVER knew that.." his laughter died as he realized what he said. I reached up to cup his face "It's okay, Nicholas." he leaned into my hand and turned his face to kiss my palm "I know. Bringing it all up, it's hard." he said "I've never told anyone about it before." he said, "Me and Lucy usually never talk about it, its hard. Our lives got taken from us by some maniac. When the new settlers came a few years later, we was lucky enough to get them to believe the land was cursed and got them to settle somewhere else." I remember reading about that. It was a few years later another settlement came to see how the one was doing. But they was all gone. There was no signs anyone had been there for years. No trace of people. Nothing.

I sat up straight and cleared my throat, I had more questions "So.." I began, he raised an eyebrow at me, having a feeling he knew where this was going "How are you able to be in the sunlight? Is this why you said you couldn't have kids? Can you eat food? What about drinks? Do you use the bathroom? How do you survive? How have you been able to live so long without people questioning you?" Nicholas laughed, as he held a hand up to halt my questions "Slow down." he told me, smiling "I'm happy to answer your questions." he said, as he took in a breath and let it out slowly "Okay, so umm the sunlight." he shrugged "I've never had a problem with it. Myth. I'm not sure why." he said shaking his head "Obviously, I can be in the sunlight. Yes, this is why I said you didn't have to worry about that night, because I can't have kids." I opened my mouth to ask other questions and he held up his hand "Let me finish the first ones here." he laughed as so did I, as I nodded my head "Let's see...Food and drinks, yes I can consume both. I can taste them just fine. They just don't satisfy me. If you know what I mean. So that goes with the bathroom questions, yes. Since I eat food and drinks, I do use the bathroom." he laughed, shaking his head at my questions as he answered the, "As for surviving and not being caught, me and Lucy made friends with the next set of settlers that came. The ones we made settle somewhere else. A family found out about us, but they were accepting of us. Ever since then, their family has helped us through the years." he told me, I perked up as he said that "You mean Rich?" I asked him, he nodded his head "Yes, Rich. His family." I gaped at the thought "Oh, wow!" I was definitely shocked. "Yeah." I thought for a moment as it went quiet between us before I thought of another question "How did you figure out you can't have kids?" I asked curiously. Obviously, I knew the answer, but I wanted to hear it from him. For the first time since meeting this man, I saw him turn red. I laughed "Come on.." I egged him on. He sighed, as he ran a hand through his hair "It was with Lucy." He said shrugging some "Yeah, I know. She wanted to experiment. She figured it was better to do with me, than someone else." he shrugged his shoulders as I gaped at him "Oh my goodness. Seriously?" I laughed as he shook his head at me "Yeah, wasn't really much of a thing as protection back then. So, we did it, a few times. And she never got pregnant." I nodded my head "Makes sense. Did you ever try with a human woman?" I asked him, he blushed again "Yes." he admitted "A woman was begging to get pregnant, I told her I couldn't help her, but she wouldn't take no for an answer. So, I tried. Many times. Then she chased me out of her house with a knife." he laughed at the memory and lifted his shirt up to show his side "That's where this scar came from." I gasped, as I reached to touch the scar. How did I not notice it? I traced it down his side "Oh, Nicholas." I said, as I looked at him. He lowered his shirt and shrugged "Hey, it didn't kill me. So, there's that." he laughed it off. I guess he was right. We sat there, this new information between us now, and I began to think. I guess he was right when he said he could take on Theo if he needed to. And as if he knew I was thinking of him, my phone chimed, a text message from the man himself;

Where are you???

"Fuck..." I muttered as I text him back quickly saying I was still out shopping "I've got to go." I told him, as I hurried to get up and headed for the door. Nicholas was so quick to get to the door before me "Abigail." I came to a halt before I walked into him "Nicholas." I said back to him "I have to go." he nodded "I know. Just..You can't tell anyone." he looked at me, pleading with me. I leaned up and kissed him gently on the lips "Your secret is safe with me." I told him with a smile, as I shoved him out of the way and opened the door "I'll get with you in a few days. I still have more questions." I said with a smile on my face "I'll be waiting!" he called after.

I hurried through a few shops to buy some things, so it didn't look like I was lying about shopping. I then called the driver and told him to meet me at my store to pick me up. Once I got there, I shoved my shopping bags into the driver's hands to deal with as I climbed into the back of the car. I jumped and yelped as Theo was sitting there "Jesus Christ." Theo smirked "Close, but no." I rolled my eyes at him "What are you doing?" I asked him "I figured we could grab dinner." he said with a charming smile. I smiled back at him "That sounds great." he motioned to the driver to leave once the guy was back in the driver seat. We headed off towards a restaurant. The rest of the night was surprisingly pleasant with Theo. Usually it was him ignoring me, but he was all about me tonight. He asked me about what I did for the day. Where I went. What I did. Which, of course, made me a little nervous, but I kept it cool and answered all his questions. He seemed satisfied with my answers. Once we had dinner, we made our way back to his house. Immediately, once inside the doors of his house, he grabbed me, picking me up. I wrapped my arms around his neck and my legs around his waist. We kissed passionately. He was stripping my shirt off of me, I was grabbing at his shirt to get it off of him. We made our way to his room, where he kicked the door shut, the rest of the night spent in his bed, passionately making love over and over again.

6

A few weeks passed before I could even get back to see Nicholas. Theo canceled a ton of appointments to "spend time with me" as he put it. But a part of me wondered if he had been suspicious of what I had really been up to when I said I went to the city to do shopping. Eventually, he couldn't cancel anymore appointments and he was gone, he said he would be gone for a couple weeks. I told him I didn't want to stay in this house alone for a couple weeks, I would be staying at my apartment. He was reluctant to let that happen, but it was going to happen whether he liked it or not. Theo gave in and agreed. But I had a feeling he was going to be having some of his men watching over me there too.

I stood in my apartment, pacing back and forth. I had text Nicholas and told him to meet me here, but he had to get in through a back way. Theo had been sitting outside, watching. I became nervous, thinking maybe they spotted him, did he have guys all over the building? It really wouldn't surprise me. When I heard the knock at my door, I jumped. I stood there for a moment, before I heard his voice "Abigail, it's Nicholas." I smiled, as I rushed to the door to unlock it and open it. Nicholas smiled at me as he walked inside the apartment. I shut and locked the door behind him "I didn't think I was ever going to see you again." I said, as I sat down on the couch. Nicholas sat down next to me, grabbing my hand and placing a tender kiss to my knuckles "I knew we would." he said with a smile. I felt my face flush, as I smiled back at him "So..." I started, but immediately losing my train of thought as we just sat there staring at each other. What was it about him that made me just go all stupid around him? I shook my head, laughing some "Is it a vampire thing to make me go all stupid around you with you staring at me like that?" Nicholas chuckled, shaking his head "Umm, no. I don't think it is. Must just be my natural charm." He winked at me in a teasing manner, causing me to laugh even more "Well, you might be right, I suppose." I had truly missed this. Nicholas just made me feel so comfortable with him, even knowing what I know, I still felt safe. Comfortable. I could really relax and just be myself with him. With Theo, I always felt on edge, I never knew what his mood was. One minute he could be loving and caring, and the next angry and a monster.

"So, what questions did you still have for me?" Nicholas prompted "Oh, yeah!" I said, remembering now why he was here. I still had questions I wanted answers to. I thought about the main one, the farm. How did he know it? Why did he know it? I fiddled with the bottom of my shirt, staring down at it, like it was going to ask the question for me. It was a tough subject, that farm was my haven. Then it became my nightmare. I finally looked up at him, sadness all over my face "How do you know about the farm?" Nicholas sighed, like it was a heavy subject for him too "It's a long story." he said, as if he was trying to get out of telling me. I debated for a moment, but I had to know "Tell me." Nicholas nodded as he agreed "Okay.." he adjusted himself to a more comfortable position before he began to speak "In about 1660s, the English took control over what would become New York the state, making it one of the original 13 colonies. Before then, it was the Dutch that had first settled there, but of course, the English couldn't have that." he chuckled, shaking his head "Anyways, me and Lucy and a few others made our way up to New York, it was about time for us to start moving on at that point. We travelled through and found a plot of land. Lucy and I settled there, we built a house, a barn, fence, traded goods for animals and seeds. We started a farm. We started a life, but we also knew we could only stay there for at most 20 years. Before people got suspicious of us. At one point a young gentleman fell in love with Lucy, but she did everything to deny him. She told him she had no interest in him, even went as far as saying I was her lover." Nicholas stared off, he wasn't really looking at anything, but you could tell he was seeing the past, he smiled, but it was sad. He laughed slightly at the memory of the young man, falling in love with Lucy "Unfortunately, the young man became very obsessed with Lucy. He snuck into our home one night, slit my throat and then tried to rape Lucy and take her for his own. The surprise on the that young man's face when I dragged him out of her room, blood dripping down my neck, he really didn't see it coming, of course." He scoffed, as he shook his head "He was the first guy I ever killed, honestly. Even when I first turned, I didn't kill anyone." he shrugged his shoulders "I just couldn't do it." he looked at me then, and smiled softly "Anyways, I killed him. We buried him deep in the woods on the farm. After a few days, one of the other vampires that travelled with us visited us with some news. They had married a human. The human knew all about them. Lucy and I was wary about it, but the way the human woman looked at him, it was hard to believe that she meant him or us any harm. And she didn't. They adopted kids throughout the years. They built a life. Eventually, it came time for Lucy and I to move on. We gave our farm to one of their kids. Mary, I think her name was. She was always loving the farm, she ran around there from the time she could walk. She helped care for the animals and everything. She had a passion about her, so it only seemed fitting to give it to her. Mary was excited, but she was sad because we was leaving. But we had to." He smiled sadly. He paused for a moment, staring at me. Then it hit me, I gasped "You're telling me, you built the farm that was my childhood escape?" Nicholas nodded his head "It really hasn't changed much over the centuries, surprisingly." he noted. I nodded my head, remembering being told that most of all the build-ings were original, the only thing that changed was a newer home had been built to preserve the original home. I smiled, thinking back to all the years I spent at that farm.

I took a deep breath and let it out slowly "One summer, right before I left to come here to the city, me and Claire were planning to take a bus and head west. We wanted to travel. We didn't want to go to college, we both had a passion for clothing and Claire was beautiful as all get out, I told her she could be a model and I would create the outfits." I felt my breath catch in my throat "Her boyfriend at the time didn't like the idea. He wanted her to stay there at the farm, to stay in the small town, while he worked some dead-end job and be his wife. Claire didn't want that." I closed my eyes, reliving that night, I felt tears swell up, I opened my eyes to look at Nicholas, as the tears fell down my face "The night we were supposed to leave, I couldn't get a hold of Claire. I ran to the farm as fast as I could, worried. I called out to her, to her parents. No one answered. I ran to the barn; I found her boyfriend. I also found Claire and her parents dead on the ground. He had killed them. Because Claire didn't want to stick around. Her parents weren't forcing her to be with the boy, they never liked him anyways. I had already called the cops before I ran over, because I knew something was wrong. I stalled the boyfriend until the cops showed up." I took a shaky breath and shook my head. Nicholas reached out to wipe the tears away. I half smiled at him, as I sniffed "That farm was my haven. My escape. My home life wasn't the greatest. Claire was like a sister to me. My best friend. And that monster took her from me. Her parents were so sweet too, they treated me like I was one of their own. Always told me I had a place in their home, no matter what." I smiled thinking of their kindness over the years of my childhood. I mourned them more than I ever did my own family. "That's why Lucy is here." he spoke quietly. I raised an eyebrow at him "What do you mean?" I asked him curiously "Well, when I heard about what happened there, the thought of the place I built going to some-one that wouldn't take care it, I couldn't do it. So, I bought it. Over the past few years, I have been working on preserving it better. Keeping it maintained. Plus, there is still animals there to take care of. I eventu-ally hired help for the animals, but my heart is in this city." he grabbed my hand and placed it on his chest over his heart. I could faintly feel it beating, which made me gasp some, he chuckled "Yeah, I have a heart-beat." he said, I smiled as I looked at him "Lucy is here, because I am signing the farm over to her. She has someone in mind that can take care of the farm and keep it going for many more years." he told me, which made my heart soar. I never kept up to date as to what had happened to the place. I had always hoped someone bought it and kept I the way it was. Hearing that Nicholas did just that made me so happy. But at the same time, my heart still ached, I wanted the whole farm to burn that night. I even debated locking the bastards inside the barn and burning it to the ground with him inside of it, but I couldn't do that to Claire and her parents. They deserved better.

We sat there in silence for a few moments as I processed over everything Nicholas told me. My mind was still reeling. I had had other questions for him, but at the moment, they were gone "Any other questions for me?" he asked, as if reading my mind, causing me to laugh "Can you read minds?" I asked him. Nicholas chuckled and shook his head "No, I can't. But I'm very good at reading faces and have great intuition. I was like that before a vampire and becoming one, just sort of enhanced it." he said with a shrug "I wasn't given a manual when I got turned. So, it was just sort of a learning process as the years went on." he said "I was thankful for Lucy though. I would have gone insane if not for her." a smile came to his face for his dear friend. And honestly, if it wasn't for Lucy being into women, I would be very jealous of her. And, if I admitted it to myself, I kind of was. Lucy had such a bond with Nicholas that I wanted so badly. But the more I thought about it, the more I realized I would die before Nicholas ever did. He even warned me about that. I was a pretty healthy woman, so I had maybe 70 years tops. Unless Theo killed me first. I went stiff at the thought. Theo would kill me if he knew I was with Nicholas this entire time while he was gone. He would even try to kill Nicholas too. I felt myself going into a panic, and Nicholas could sense it. He pulled me into a hug, holding me close. He rested his head on top of mine, gently rubbing my back "I promise I won't ever let any kind of harm come to you, Abigail." He told me and I truly believed it. I knew Nicholas would keep me safe. I knew he would protect me, no matter what. But I also knew Theo wanted me to himself and he would do whatever it took to make sure I was only with him, no one else could have me and I had a gut feeling that if Theo couldn't have me, then no one could and that meant killing me to keep me away from any other man.

Nicholas and I spent the next couple weeks really getting to know each other. He stayed at my apartment with me, and we never left it the entire time. I ordered food in; we watched tons of movies and TV shows. He even invited Lucy over for a couple nights and we all had fun. It was probably the best two weeks of my life. It ended abruptly, as I laid there in bed, naked with Nicholas. His body was draped over mine. I just laid there in content, gently stroking his back when my phone went off. Ignored it at first, but it kept going off. Then eventually it began to ring. I huffed in frustration as I grabbed my phone and my heart stopped when I saw Theo calling "Hello?" I answered, I went stiff, my heart pounding. Nicholas felt the change in my body and my heart pounding, he woke up ready to fight. But when he saw I was on the phone, he went silent. "Abby, I'm heading home right now. You better be there waiting." it was all Theo said before he hung up. I gaped at the phone and sighed. I looked at Nicholas, he looked even more handsome when he woke up. His eyes were light and sweet. His hair was messy. I moved to position myself on my knees, I wrapped my arms up around his neck, his arms went around my waist, pulling me closer. I laughed, as I kissed his lips, he softly kissed me back. I sighed, as I pulled away and rest my forehead against his "I have to go." I said quietly. Nicholas nodded his head, he knew just as I did, this time was going to come to an end, but neither of us liked it. I pulled away from him and made my way to the bathroom to get a quick shower and dress. When I came out, Nicholas was already dressed and standing out in the main area of the apartment. I slipped on some shoes, grabbed my purse and made sure I had everything I needed. Who knew when I would be back in my apartment? It was becoming my new secret haven. I sighed, as I opened the door to leave and stood there for a moment. I didn't want to leave. I felt tears well up in my eyes, I quickly blinked them away. I shut the door and locked it behind me. I turned to head down the hallway, but Nicholas stopped me. He pulled me close to him and kissed me as if he was never going to get the chance to do it again. And honestly, I didn't blame him. I didn't know when I would see him again. If Theo found out about this, he would kill me. Then hunt Nicholas down and try to kill him too. I sighed as we pulled away from each other. He reluctantly let go of me "I promise I will get you out of this, Abigial." I believed him, but it was hard to imagine it. I smiled at him as he went one way and I went the other. I got outside of the apartment building and surprisingly enough, there was a driver waiting. I rolled my eyes, as I got inside of the car, and we made our way to Theo's house.

As promised, I was there waiting when Theo arrived home. I was pacing back and forth in one of the dens when he came barging inside. He startled me, causing me to stop and jump a bit "Jesus.." I muttered, as he stalked towards me. He pulled him roughly to him, kissing me hard. I squirmed, trying to force him off of me "Theo!" I was able to say, as I got my mouth away from his, but his lips just trailed down my neck. I kept trying to shove him "Get off of me!" he finally listened, I was able to shove him away. I shook my head, a look of disgust on my face at him "I'm done with you, Theo." I told him, standing my ground. "I'm tired of being your little pet. I'm tired of you bossing me around and thing you can tell me what to do and I will obey. Enough is enough. I am a person. A human being." I felt confident in my words, but the look upon his face was making it hard to stand my ground. He looked like he could just strangle me, and he looked like he wanted to "Is this so?" he said through clenched teeth, it caused me to hesitate and that was enough for him. He grinned at me, chuckling "Oh, Abby." he said, stepping closer to me. He ran a hand through my hair before grabbing a fist full of it and yanking hard. I let out a scream of pain, closing my eyes "You are mine. You belong to me and only me. The only way out of this is if I get bored or, well...you really don't want to the other option." he chuckled evilly, and it made chills run down my spine.

Theo kept a hold of my hair in his fist and dragged me over to chair in the den, he bent me over the arm of it, shoving me hard against it, causing me to gasp to catch my breath. I groaned, as pain shot through my stomach "Theo, please.." I begged, he was hurting me, and I wasn't enjoying it at all. Theo ignored me, as he pushed down my pants and underwear. He undid his and dropped them down around his ankles. He was hard and ready, he shoved himself hard inside of me, I let out a scream, it hurt, and he took full pleasure in it. He thrust hard over and over again, I begged him to stop, but he kept going. He stopped after a moment, he pulled himself out of me, I thought maybe he was done, but instead I felt a cold liquid hit my butt hole and my eyes went wide "Theo, please. Don't!" I begged him, trying my hardest to get out of his grip. He held tight to my hair still, causing my more pain on my head "This is your punishment, Abby." he growled out, as he rubbed the tip of his penis against my butt hole. I whimpered as he slowly shoved himself inside, I had hoped he would be gentle, but he wasn't. He shoved hard and I let out a cry. He thrust hard and fast, I cried harder, but that only seemed to fuel his pleasure more and more. He gripped my hip hard with his free hand, keeping a tight hold of my hair still. I begged him to stop, but he kept going. Eventually, I stopped asking, I let the tears slide down my face silently, I bit my lip so hard, it was bleeding. Theo came with a growl and thrust as hard as he could. I whimpered when he pulled out. I was panting from the pain of it all, he let go of me finally and I slumped to the ground by the chair. I pulled my legs up to my chest and wrapped my arms around them burying my face. I cried more. Theo bent down and grabbed my hair, pulling my face up to look at him, I winced at the pain "Next time, I will fill all 3 holes and fuck you senseless, over and over and over." fear filled my face as I stared at him, I didn't want that. As much as I enjoyed kinky, hard rough sex, this wasn't it. It was meant to be enjoyable for both parties, not just one. He let my head drop and I buried my face again, I listened as he walked out of the door and slammed the door shut hard behind him. I jumped at the sound and cried harder. I had to get out of here. I had to get away from him. I didn't want Theo. I wanted Nicholas, after spending two glorious weeks with him, I knew in my heart, mind and soul, it was Nicholas. He was the one I was meant to be with. Even if I would die before he ever did, it didn't matter. It would be the best damn years of my life. Sniffing, I wiped the tears from my face. I winced as I stood up, I put back on my underwear and pants. I made my way to one of the many bedrooms that had it's own bathroom. I locked the door and went into the bathroom where I locked the door as well. I turned on the shower water to get it ready. I stripped from my clothes and noticed the blood in my underwear from my butt. I sighed, as I tossed the underwear into the trash. I stood there, staring at myself in the mirror. Just a few hours away, I was so happy. Now, I was terrified. I grabbed my phone and pulled up the messages between Nicholas and I.

Nicholas, I have to get away from him. I have to leave him. I can't do this. He will kill me.

I sent the message. I waited for a reply, and it came quickly;

Don't worry about it. I've got you.

I smiled at the words. I sighed, as I set my phone down and got into the shower. I took my time showering. I was very sore. I sighed into the warm water, just standing there. I got lost in my own thoughts, thinking about a life with Nicholas. Would we adopt kids like his friends did? Did he even want kids? Did I even want kids? My hands went to my stomach, I wasn't sure I ever did. With the life I had growing up, I always had a fear of turning into my parents. But I did everything in my power to separate myself from that life. I was always kind to little kids. I even volunteered a few times at a kid's home. I always donated to them whenever I could. I sighed as I dropped my hands. I would never carry a child. Nicholas couldn't have kids. But I knew I loved him. *Love.* I thought. It made me smile. I love Nicholas. It made me smile even more. I had to see him. I had to tell him to his face. I turned the water off to the shower and wringed out my hair. I stepped out of the shower, wrapping a towel around my body and around my hair. I reached for my phone to text Nicholas, but it was gone. I frowned, as I looked around and gasped when I was Theo. He held my phone in his hand and shook it back and forth "Looking for this?" he asked, my first thought was how the hell did he even get in here "Yes, but how did you get in here?" I asked him, he smirked "This is my home, Abby." he held up a key in the other hand, I frowned at him "Okay. Well, I'd like some privacy and my phone back, please." I was trying hard to not give him attitude. Theo shook his head, as he unlocked my phone and it opened right to her messages with Nicholas "It seems you have been very busy." he said, tsking at me, as if I was a child being bad "Looks like you and this Nicholas guy are planning on running away? Maybe even trying to kill me?" he asked. My eyes went wide, I shook my head at him "Theo, no! I would never plan to kill you." I told him, but I wanted to leave, I did want to run away with Nicholas "You can't just keep me to yourself." I told him, Theo thought that was funny, he dropped my phone to the ground and stomped on it, crushing it "That's what you think." He said in a dark, sinister voice. I felt fear sweep through me, causing a chill to run down my spine. Theo launched at me, I screamed and the next thing I knew, everything went black.

7

"Abby..Wake up!" I stirred for a moment, before slowly blinking my eyes open. It was bright, the sun was shining through a window, a breeze was fluttering the curtain softly. I lay there, confused, as I glanced around. I knew this room. "Abigail Nicole Baker.." a loud pounding on the door made me jump up into a sitting position "Wake up this instant." more pounding. I felt my heart pounding just as hard as the person pounding on the door. But wait, I knew that voice too. *No, it couldn't be..* I thought as I glanced around. Sure enough, I was in my childhood bedroom. It was my mother pounding on the door to wake me up. I quickly jumped from the bed and opened the bedroom door "Sorry, mother. I'm awake." My mother, a thin fragile looking woman, with brown, curly hair that always looked like it was cooked way to long with a blow dryer. She always had it kept up in a messy bun. She always wore the same baggy shirts and biker shorts. She stood there with a hand on her hip, hip cocked to one side, glaring down at me as if I was a pest in her house that was bothering her "You have chores to get done." she sneered at me before she turned and walked away. I sighed, nodding my head "Yes, ma'am." I mumbled, as I left my bedroom, I used the bathroom really quick before I got started on the chores.

I started in the living room, cleaning up things. I grabbed the sweeper and began to sweep the floors. Something from the TV caught my attention. It was a man, why did he look familiar. I stopped sweeping and just stood there staring at the man. My mother hit me with the folded-up newspaper like a dog "Get back to work!" she shouted, causing me to startle. I shook my head and went back to sweeping. I swore I kept hearing my name being called, but there was no one there but me and my mother. I just ignored it. I continued cleaning. Hours later, I finally finished. I asked my mother if it was okay to head over to Claire's. She shrugged and waved me off. I happily ran out of the house and down the road. When I got to Claire's house I came to a stop. Her house was gone. Only the old original house was left. I frowned, as I walked slowly towards it. I walked up the porch and knocked on the door "Hello!" I called out. There was silence, I knocked again, and the door pushed open. I hesitated for a moment before I pushed the door open even more. I stepped inside, and glanced around "Hello, Claire?" I called out. I sighed, when no one appeared or called back. I was about to leave when I hear my name again "Hello?!" I called out, I heard my name whispered again. I felt a chill run down my spine, I turned to quickly leave, but ran into a body. I gasped, as I stumbled backwards "Abigail, you have to wake up!" the man from the TV yelled at me. He tried to grab me, but he couldn't reach me. Why did he seem so familiar? I tried to reach for him too, but it was like the space between us kept getting farther and farther apart. "Abigail, please! Wake up!!" I felt tears stream down my face "I am awake!" I called after him "I am awake!"

I came awake with a start, I groaned as I grabbed at my head, feeling a bump on the side of my head. I mumbled under my breath, trying to remember what had happened. I glanced around, I wasn't sure where I was at. My hair felt damp under my hand, and it clicked, I was showering. I had just got out when Theo came in. He found my phone and went through my messages then he attacked me. Sighing, I stood up, it was dark. It smelled moldy, I could hear water dripping somewhere, I wasn't sure, it was echoing. I sighed, as I blinked my eyes a few times, trying to get them to adjust to the darkness. I looked around, I saw a faint light go past what I figured was windows, was it headlights from a car? It almost looked like I was in an old warehouse of some sort. I glanced down, thankful that Theo at least put clothes on me. I wrapped my arounds around me, there was a chill to the air, and I was cold from laying on the damp concrete floor. "Theo!?" I called out, maybe he was still around. "Theo! Come on, let's...let's talk about this!" I sighed when there was no answer. I debated what to do, I wasn't even sure where I was at. But if I could get to people, then I could get to help.

Suddenly, I heard the noise of an old door opening. I stood still. I could make out the faint shape of a body, it made its way towards me. My heart pounded heavily in my chest and ears. Finally, the person got close enough to see it was Theo. I took a few steps back away from him, he chuckled "Abby, Abby, Abby." he tsked at me. "We have ourselves an issue, don't we." I stared him down, I was ready to fight, I wouldn't go down without a fight. "Theo, just let me go. You don't have to do this." I told him, He scoffed at me "Oh, but I do, Abby. You were to only be mine. And now you've been tainted by another man." He reached into the waistband of his pants and pulled out a knife. I gasped, frantically searching the area around me, hoping that maybe there would be something I could grab to protect myself with, but there wasn't. "Theo, please." I begged him, feeling tears fill my eyes "To late, Abby." he said, as he lunged towards me. I let out a scream and ran as fast as I could. Theo was to quick though, he grabbed me and pulled me tight against him. He placed on hand at my mouth and the knife at my throat "It's time to say goodby, Abby." he laughed in my ear, I kicked as hard backwards as I could, he let out a groan and let me go "I don't think so, Theo." I punched him as hard as I could in the face, he dropped the knife and grabbed at his face, cussing me out. My eyes went wide, I grabbed for the knife, right as he grabbed for me. I felt the knife plunge into him, but at the same time, I felt something hit me too. I gasped, as I stared up at him "Don't think it would be so easy, Abby, dear." he smiled, as he twisted a knife into my gut. I gasped, as I fell back away from him. He kept a hold of the knife in his hand and pulled the one from his side out. He hissed, as he watched me fall to my knees. He smirked, feeling satisfied "Rot here for all eternity, Abigial." He turned to leave and the last sound I heard was the sound of the door slamming shut and locking. I began to hyper-ventilate. I could taste blood in my mouth, I swayed there on my knees, before falling backwards onto the cold concrete floor.

As I laid there, the life literally draining from my body, it wasn't my life that flashed before my eyes. It was, *"how the fuck did I get to this point?"* My vision was becoming blurry, I was getting colder as I lay on that cold concrete floor. Why did I believe he loved me? Why did I think even for one tiny moment I meant something real to him?

My breath catches a bit in my throat as I inhale. I slowly exhale and find it harder to breathe. I can faintly hear noises in the distance, sounds like shouting, screaming. Fighting. I'm not sure. I'm starting to lose consciousness. My eyes slowly begin to shut, I think to myself *"This is it. This is how it ends. In an abandoned building. Alone. Bleeding out."* I feel a single tear slide down my cheek. I want to reach up to brush it away, but my arms feel so heavy.

When I feel like the end is near, I take one deep breath and let it out slowly. I hear a voice. My name? Is someone talking to me? Is someone there? I'm not sure. I try to open my eyes, but they won't. I try to move but I can't. I suddenly feel arms wrapped around me, shaking me. I can hear them screaming my name, but it sounds muffled. My last thought was *"At least I won't die alone."*

I awoke with a start. I slowly opened my eyes, blinking a few times. I could hear beeping and other odd noises. I wasn't sure what they were. I glanced around and wasn't sure where I was. I furrowed my eyebrows in confusion before I realized I was in a hospital bed, in a hospital room. "Abigail." I jumped at the sound of my voice, I turned towards where it came from, and relief filled me when I saw Nicholas. I felt tears fill my eyes "Nicholas." I tried to move, but immediately was greeted with a bunch of pain. I winced at it and grabbed at my stomach "Hey. Don't move. Okay. You just had surgery." He moved closer to me and grabbed my hand, lifting it up to kiss it gently. I smiled at him, but then fear filled me "Theo?" I asked, Nicholas shook his head "You never have to worry about him ever again." he told me, I nodded my head as I settled back down into the bed. I sat there quietly for a moment, I was ready to ask Nicholas some questions when the Doctor knocked and walked in "Oh, hey. Glad to see you awake." the woman smiled, I half smiled back to her "Thanks. Me too." I said, though right now, I'd rather be passed back out than to deal with this pain "How are you feeling?" the Doctor asked, as she began to go through checking my vitals "I feel like I got ran over by a train." I told her, the Doctor half smiled and nodded her head "I would say so. How is the pain?" she asked me as she stood by my bed "I'd give it a 20." I told her, the Doctor chuckled and nodded her head "That's normal. I'll get you some more pain meds. In the meantime, take it easy. We want to keep you over for one more night, just to keep an eye on you. Otherwise, you will be good to go in the morning." I smiled at the Doctor and nodded my head "That sounds good to me." The Doctor nodded her head "Great. Get some rest and hopefully we will have you out of here in no time." the Doctor smiled softly at us both before she left. I sighed deeply before I turned to Nicholas "Thank you. For every-thing." he shook his head, as he leaned in to kiss my forehead "I would die ten thousand times over before I ever let you die." I leaned into him, closing my eyes. At least Theo wouldn't be an issue anymore. I just had to heal and get better.

Laying there motionless for what felt like hours, Theo finally stirred. He growled as he struggled a bit to stand up, but once he did, he rolled his shoulders and cracked a few bones to put them back into place. He laughed evilly "Oh, Nicholas. Now I remember you. You showed me who you truly are, now I'm going to show you who I truly am." Theo dusted himself off, but realized he definitely needed to get a change of clothes. He called for his driver and hopped in. The driver looked puzzled at the way he looked "Don't ask questions." the driver nodded and just drove Theo home. Once there, he made his way inside. He took a quick shower and changed his clothes. Those wounds were healing nicely, but they would definitely leave scars. He growled at the thought of his perfect body being marked up. But that was okay, he was going to get his revenge. He stared at his reflection in the mirror grinned "Nicholas, you will watch me as I tear that little bitch piece by piece. Then you will devour her. Then I am going to fucking kill you. For good this time." Theo laughed evilly at his plan. He would be done with them both, for good.

8

It was about a month after the whole incident. I was slowly getting back to normal. I was still a bit sore, but I was getting better every day. Nicholas had moved into my apartment for the time being, but I was slowly trying to convince him to just completely move here. He was teasing me about all his stuff, but I think secretly he was going too. Despite everything, I was happy. Nicholas would help me walk down the stairs to get outside to walk around the neighborhood for a bit, he helped me shower, he helped me dress, he helped with whatever he thought I needed help with. I honestly loved it. I had never had some-one care so much about me for so long. I felt loved. And as we sat there one night, eating dinner, I just stared across the table at him, just smiling. He looked up at me, stopped mid bite and laughed "What?" he asked, before he actually took a bite. I laughed and shook my head, before I became serious. "I love you, Nicholas." I told him, wondering if I should of said it. It took him aback, he stared at me for a moment, before he stood up, got on his knees in front of me. He grabbed both of my hands and lifted them up to kiss them "I love you, Abigial." he said with a smile. I smiled back to him, as I wrapped my arms around him and leaned in to give him a kiss. He lifted me up out of the chair, I wrapped my legs around his waist, but winced "Oh..yeah. Still healing." I rolled my eyes. Nicholas laughed, as he gently carried me over to the couch and gently sat me down. I sighed as I leaned into him. My life was perfect right now, there was nothing that could make it any better and I really didn't think there was anything that could take this feeling away.

A few more weeks passed; I was almost completely better. I could definitely walk around more without needing much, I could do a lot without needing Nicholas's help. I had told him if he wanted to go back to his apartment, he was welcome to. He shrugged his shoulders and simply told me all of his belongings were in storage and he had already leased out the apartment to someone else. I was so happy that he was telling me he was staying with me in my apartment. I finally wanted to make a trip over to my store. It had been so long since I had been there. Were the people Theo had hired still running it? Was it even still there? I wasn't even sure. But Nicholas agreed he would ride over with me. Once there, the shop was open. Nicholas told me he had to run down to a store to grab a few things, he promised he would be quick. I smiled, gave him a kis and told him I'd see him in a few.

I stepped inside and one of the girls working, happily smiled at me "Oh, Abigial!" she said, I raised an eyebrow at her, she looked familiar, but I wasn't sure "Hey." I said, waving slightly "I just wanted to check to make sure everything was going good." the girl nodded her head "Oh yeah, it's going great! We were just putting out new shipment of items." I nodded my head "Okay. So, everything going well?" the girl nodded again "Yes, Theo said we were fine to keep working here. But unless you want your store back…" the girl trailed off, my face went white as a ghost *Theo??* There was no way. "When…When did you speak with Theo?" I asked her, the girl smiled "Oh, just the other day." My heart sank, I thought I was going to pass out. I tried to make it seem like I was fine, I calm and cool that it was normal for a man that was supposed to be dead walking around the living "Oh, okay. Yeah, that is fine." I told the girl "Umm, I've gotta go." I turned quickly and left the shop, I turned to go down the block and ran right straight into Nicholas "Jesus.." I muttered but grabbing hold of him and not letting go. He could tell by my face that something was wrong "What happened? What is it?" he was on alert, looking all around us "He's alive." I told him, Nicholas looked confused as he looked down at me

"Who?" he asked, "Theo." I could barely get the name out, as I choked and felt the tears fall down my face. Nicholas laughed and shook his head "That is impossible." I frowned at him "No kidding, but the girl at the shop said she just talked to him the other day." Nichloas frowned down at me "Maybe it was someone else." I rolled my eyes at him "But why would someone pretend to be him?" I asked him, he shrugged his shoulders. "I don't know, Abigial, but there is no way he could still be alive unless..." he trailed off his words and I didn't like the look upon his face, I had a feeling we were thinking the same thing "Vampire.." I whispered the word out. We both looked around before we hailed a cab down to get back home. Once we were back to the apartment, Nicholas began to pace back and forth, constantly checking the window to the street down below. I watched him be this way for almost an hour before I stepped in front of him and stopped him from pacing. He almost knocked me over, because he wasn't paying attention "Why don't we go back to where you left him?" I offered, but Nicholas shook his head "No, I don't think that would be a good idea." I frowned and then sighed, as I sat down on the couch "What do we do?" Nicholas sighed, feeling defeated, he wasn't sure. He knew he had to find Theo and end it once and for all, but he couldn't drag Abigial into it again. She had already suffered so much by this man; he couldn't ask her to come along. But then again, he knew she would come whether he wanted her to or not. Maybe he would have to sneak out after she went to bed. Nicholas looked at Abigial and smiled sweetly at her, he cupped her face in his hand and brushed his thumb gently across her cheek. His sweet Abigail. He would die a thousand times over to make sure she was kept safe. He knew what he had to do, even if it meant lying to Abigial. He gently kissed her, wondering if this would be the last time, he saw her. Because if he failed in killing Theo, Nicholas knew that Theo wouldn't hesitate to kill him, then come after Abigial too. He cherished this small moment with her, memorized her face and features, because by tomorrow, who knew what would happen.

I lay there in bed with Nicholas, I couldn't sleep. All I could think about was Theo. What if he tried to come in the middle of the night and kill us while we slept. Every little noise I heard; I kept thinking it was Theo. I sighed, as I closed my eyes and tried to sleep. But I couldn't. I felt Nicholas move and get out of bed, I just assumed maybe he was getting a drink or using the bathroom, I laid there waiting for him to come back, but he never did. I gave it a few more minutes before I got out of bed myself and looked for him. I checked every room in the apartment, Nicholas was gone. I frowned, why would he leave? I plopped onto the couch and noticed a little black box sitting on top of a note. I raised an eyebrow as I grabbed the little box and read the note:

Abigial,

I am so sorry to have to do this. I love you with every fiber of my being, but to keep you safe, I have to do this. I must protect you. I must end this. And I cannot do it if you are next to me. Please do not come looking for me. I will return. I promise. Open the little box. Keep it safe for me until I return.

Love you,

Nicholas.

I felt tears well up in my eyes, as I sat the note down and opened the box. I gasped when I saw it was a beautiful ring. It was a 2 carat Princess Cut Diamond ring, set on a band of diamonds on a silver band. I slipped the ring onto my finger, it fit so perfectly, and it looked so beautiful there. I felt the tears fall down my face, as I hugged my hand to my chest "Oh, Nicholas. Why?" I spoke quietly to the empty apartment. Theo would kill him. Then come and kill me. I sobbed quietly for a moment, before wiping away the tears. I had to go find Nicholas, I had to help him. Whether he wanted it or not, I couldn't let him die.

It took me only a moment to figure out that Theo was probably hiding out at his home. Where else would he hole up for a bit to plan out a killing? I hailed a cab and made my way there. I had the cab driver stop half a mile from his home. The cab driver seemed curious about it but didn't question it when I paid him and gave him a rather large tip. I thanked him and shut the door and waited till he drove away. I tucked my hands into my coat pocket and quietly made my way up the road towards Theo's home. I slipped around the side of the house, following along the tall bushes he had planted for privacy. I had spent plenty of time here, I knew where there were ways to get in and out of this house without even being seen. And I had seen others do it too. I stopped by the bushes and waited a moment, as I heard rustling. I thought maybe a guard was on duty, I went to go peek through the bushes, but suddenly I was grabbed, and a hand placed over my mouth to keep me from screaming. I stared up at Nicholas who was ready to rip my throat out. He had his teeth and fangs bared at me, his eyes were dark, but with a shine to them that showed he was a predator and deadly. He relaxed just a bit when he saw it was me, but then realized it was me, here at Theo's and he became tense "What are you doing here?" he whispered angrily to me. He slowly moved his hand from my mouth, as I frowned at him, putting my hands on my hips "What are *you* doing here?" I asked back "How could you leave me, nonetheless, leave me a note." He stood there quietly, and sighed "I'm sorry, Abigail, I was trying to prevent this." he gestured to me being here "You need to leave." I shook my head, standing my ground "No. I'm here and I'm staying. You're not doing this alone." I knew I was being stubborn, because how the hell was I supposed to fight down a vampire? Nicholas sighed, knowing that he wasn't going to get any- where with me. He reached behind him and pulled out a sharp knife and handed it to me "You get the chance, stab his heart." I nodded my head as I took the knife, Nicholas motioned for me to follow him. We quietly made our way through the yard and got into the house. It was eerily quiet. I didn't like it; I felt a chill run down my spine. I tugged at Nicholas' shirt, he turned to look at me "This doesn't feel right." I whispered to him. He nodded his head in agreement. We stood there in a dark room for a moment, before we heard movement behind us. We both spun around, and Nicholas was hit hard and thrown against a wall hard "Nicholas!" I screamed. Theo held Nicholas against the wall, laughing darkly "Well, well, well. What do we have here?" he smirked as he looked back and forth between us "You saved me the work of snatching this little bitch up." He laughed, as he pressed harder against Nicholas's throat, I could hear him finding it hard to breath "Theo, please! You have me. Let Nicholas go. You can have me!" I quickly hid the knife in the band at the back of pants, trying to reason with the manic. Theo laughed and shook his head "Oh, I don't think so. Nicholas here is going to watch as I tear you apart, piece by piece. Then I'm going to make him devour you. Then I'm going to rip his heart out and eat." Theo laughed manically, I felt my eyes go wide, as fear consumed me. Theo was a monster. A real life monster. He pushed Nicholas hard against the wall, knocking him down before he turned to grab me. I tried to escape, but he grabbed me so quickly. I gasped, as he pulled my back up against him and he held me tight, he gripped my neck hard, almost cutting off my air flow.

Nicholas coughed as he stood up, he growled as he stared Theo down. Theo tsked at him "Now, now, Nicholas, one wrong more and her pretty little neck snaps in half." Nicholas didn't like that, He glare at the man, but didn't move "Good boy." Theo said with a chuckle, he bent down to sniff at my neck and give it a tender kiss "Mmm, I best you taste as good as you smell." he growled against my ear. I tried to move away from him, but his hold was tight and strong. He laughed as he looked at Nicholas "Tell me you've tasted her, Nicholas. Tell me she tastes as sweet as she smells. I bet she does." Theo licked my neck, I cringed, wanting so much to get away from this monster. "Come on, Nicholas, let's have a taste. You know you want to. It has to be so tempting to not taste this sweet, juicy blood flowing so warmly through her body." Theo bends my head, so my neck was more exposed, I stared at Nicholas, as he stared at my exposed neck. I was hoping he wasn't thinking about it. It never did occur to me how he got his blood supply, I never asked. And he never asked me to give him any. "Nicholas, don't listen to him!" I yelled, but Theo growled at me "Shut up!" he told me, sneering at me "Come on, Nicholas, just a small taste." Theo bared his fangs, ready to bite down onto my neck, I let out a scream, as I felt his fangs scrap my skin and then sink in, without thinking, I jerked my elbow back into his stomach as hard as I could,

Theo gasped as he let go of me and I hurried away from him. Nicholas shook his head as he reached for me and pulled me to him. I pressed my hand to my neck, feeling the blood dripping down between my fingers "Are you okay?" Nicholas asked me, I nodded my head "Yeah." he stared at me, and I saw his eyes change again, I didn't like it "Nicholas..Don't." I told him. He sniffed the air, smelling my blood, a shiver ran down his body "Abigial, you need to leave." he told me through gritted teeth. A flashback from the balcony that one night came to my memory, my eyes went wide "I'm not leaving you." I said softly. Nicholas shoved me, "Go!" he roared, I ran as fast as I could, never looking back, but it was too late; Theo had pounced on me and knocked me to the ground. I let out a scream, as he rolled me over. He was on top of me, holding my arms down to the ground above my head "Where do you think you are going?" He asked me, laughing. Nicholas ran towards us, but came to a stop, seeing me laying there, trying to get free of Theo, but all he could think about was the sweet blood coming from her neck. He had tasted it that night on the balcony and ever since then, he wanted more and more of it. It took everything he had the night he found her gutted on the warehouse floor to not devour her right there. And damnit, he wasn't going to do it tonight. He growled s he shoved Theo off of her "Leave her alone!" he roared, as he charged after the man. He was ending this once and for all.

I scurried to get up off the ground and get out of their way, I hid behind a big desk and stayed there watching the men fight like wild animals. I didn't know what to do, I wanted to help, but I knew it was useless, I would never survive out there between the two of them. I searched the room to see if there was something I could possibly grab to maybe try to knock Theo out. When I saw a bust on a pedestal, I figured it was the best I could do. I snuck over to it and grabbed it down; it was definitely heavy. I waited until Nicholas had Theo down on the ground, choking him, and I ran over with it and smashed it down on Theo's head. Nicholas jumped back; he wasn't expecting that at all. Hopefully Theo wasn't either. We both just stood there for a moment, breathing heavily. Nicholas was still in beast mode as he looked at me, I went frozen as fear came over me, I had never seen him look so mean. He looked like the monster they tell you Vampires are. And it terrified me. He started moving slowly towards me, I began to back away "Nicholas, don't." I begged him, but he wasn't listening. My neck was still bleeding some and before I could even begin to run, Nicholas had a hold of me, he pulled me tight him, burying his face into my neck and licking the blood. He growled against my skin; it sent shivers down my spine. I felt his fangs graze my skin "Nicholas, please. Don't." I begged him, as tears ran down my face, I tried desperately to shove him away from me, but he wouldn't budge, it was like trying to push a brick wall. He froze there, with his face buried against my neck, breathing heavily "Do it, Nicholas, do it!" Theo rose up from the ground, his face disfigured from the bust I had smashed down on him, I let out a scream as Nicholas held tight to me "Bite her, suck her dry!" Theo laughed evilly and at first, I thought Nicholas was going to do it, he gently kissed my neck and whispered so only I could hear it "I love you." He shoved me away, grabbing the knife tucked at the back of my pants, before turning around, letting out a warrior's yell as he plunged the knife deep into Theo's chest. Theo's eyes went wide as he saw Nicholas standing there, pushing the knife deep to the hilt and twisting it "I'll see you in hell." he told Theo, before shoving him away. Theo grabbed at the knife, shaking his head "No..NO!" he screamed, as he fell to his knees. The color from his skin began to turn pale he looked to Nicholas, and with his finally breath he spoke "I killed her. I devoured her until there was nothing left." he let out a gasped, as he collapsed on the floor. He looked like a mummified body.

We both just stood there, I was confused by what Theo had said. But Nicholas was as white as a sheet "Nicholas.." I said quietly, I slowly moved towards him, I gently touched his arm. He jumped a bit, he must forget where he was. He looked down at me, tears filled his eyes "He was the rogue vampire." He muttered as he looked down at the decayed body of Theo. I gasped as I looked at him for a moment before looking away. "Are you sure?" I asked him, Nicholas nodded "It makes sense." he sniffed as he wiped away the tears that began to fall down his face. He sighed, as he looked at me. He tilted my head gently to check my neck. At least it stopped bleeding. He rubbed the marks with his thumb "I'm so sorry, Abigial." He told me, I smiled at him, placing my hand over his on my neck "It's okay. I forgive you." he shook his head "You shouldn't be with someone like me. I'm a danger to you. I could have killed you tonight." he pleaded with me "Nicholas, if you didn't kill me when I was bleeding out from being stabbed, I don't think you ever will." I told him, as I wrapped my arms up around his neck, to pull him closer to me "I know you would never hurt me." he wrapped his arms around my waist and held me close. He kissed me gently before resting his forehead against mine "I will always protect you. Forever." he whispered. "We need to get out of here." he said, with a sigh as he pulled away from me. I frowned as I looked down at Theo before looking back at him "What do we do about him?" Nicholas fumbled in his pocket before pulling out a lighter "Fire works great of getting rid of evidence." he suggested. I shrugged my shoulders. I wasn't sure what else to do "You get home, I'll meet you there. Okay?" he kissed me gently, before shoving me slightly to get out "Okay." I told him as I disappeared from the house and walked a few ways down the road. I walked until I reached a busy section of the neighborhood and hailed down a cab. I rode in the cab all the way home, hoping that Nicholas would be careful and get back home safely.

I paced the apartment, just waiting for Nichols to show up when he finally walked through the door. I practically ran and threw myself at him. I wrapped my legs around his waist and kissed him passionately. He held me tight, kissing me back with just as much passion. He carried me over to the couch and sat down with me straddling his lap. I kissed his face all over, before kissing down his neck and nipping gently. He sucked his breath in, hissing at the pleasure it brought him. Nicholas moved his hands down to my butt and squeezed them, causing me to giggle. He laughed, as he nuzzled my neck and began to give it little kisses "I love you so much, Nicholas." I sighed out happily. He placed his hands on either side of my face, staring deeply at me "I love you so much, Abigail." he gently kissed me, I felt like butter in his hands. He kept a hold of me, as he stood up from the couch and carried me off to the bedroom, where we made hours of love, taking the time to explore every single inch of each other's bodies. Almost dying had us both craving each other badly.

Epilogue

After everything that had happened and things settled down, Nicholas properly proposed to me. He planned the whole evening. A night at a fancy restaurant first, then a peaceful walk through the park where he found the perfect spot to pop the question. I said yes to him. We immediately began to plan our little wedding. I told him he had to invite Lucy; I knew how much she meant to him. We hired someone to ordain the wedding and we did a simple little wedding in the springtime up in the countryside. It was just me, Nicholas and Lucy. It was perfect. We didn't need anyone else. We had no one else. But it didn't matter. We had each other and it was perfect. Once married, we slipped away to our apartment, we made passionate love together all night long. As we laid there in bed after round 4 or 5, I had lost count, I began to think about our future. I would grow old. Nicholas wouldn't. I would die. Nicholas wouldn't. I couldn't imagine living life without him. I sat up in bed, Nicholas adjusted himself, so he was laying on his side, with his elbow propped on the bed and his head resting in his hand. I stared down at him, smiling "Change me." he raised an eyebrow at me, confused as to what I was saying "What?" I laughed at him "Change me. Make me a vampire." his eyes went wide as he sat up in the bed, shaking his head "Abigial, no." he got serious. I frowned "Come on, Nicholas. I want to be with you forever." he sighed "I want to be with you forever to. But this..this is truly, forever. It never ends unless someone does." he shook his head "I'm sorry, Abigail, I can't do that. I can't turn you." I frowned at him, crossing my arms over my chest "Fine, I'll call Lucy. She told me she would do it, if you wouldn't." He gaped at me "No, you wouldn't." I shrugged my shoulders as I grabbed my phone and dialed Lucy, I put her on speaker phone. She answered right away "Lucy, Nicholas won't turn me. You want to do it?" Lucy let out a squeal of excitement "Yes! I'm on my way." she hung up. I smiled at Nicholas, who didn't look thrilled at all "Abigial, you don't know what you are doing." I waved him off, as I got out of the bed and began to get dressed "Lucy already told me everything I need to know. I'll be fine." he looked dumbfounded at me; he couldn't believe I had been planning this behind his back. Lucy had told me that he wouldn't do it, and that she would if he wouldn't, plus that would probably make him do it anyways. I really wanted Nicholas to do it, it would make our bond so much more if he did it, but I was understanding if he couldn't.

Before I knew it, Lucy was there. I buzzed her into the building and waited for her to get upstairs to my apartment door. I let her inside and we gave each other a hug. She smiled at Nicholas who came out of the bedroom, putting on a shirt "So, he won't do it?" I shook my head, frowning "Nope." Lucy just shrugged her shoulders "Okay." she sat on the couch and patted the spot next to her for me to sit down. I sat down next to her "Okay, Abby, you just have to relax. Be calm. Okay." I nodded my head. Lucy glanced at Nicholas who glared at her "Don't do it." Lucy shrugged as she bit onto her wrist to draw blood, she began to lift her wrist up to my mouth, when Nicholas intervened "Stop." he said sternly, sighing as he shoved Lucy away "You will be the death of me." he told me, with a little smile to his face. I beamed at him, giving him a little kiss "Thank you." I told him "Don't thank me yet." he said, as he sighed, he bit onto his wrist to draw blood "Drink." he told me, as he pressed his wrist to my mouth, I sucked the blood in. I thought it would taste weird, but it didn't. He let me suck the blood for a moment, before he pulled away. I licked at the blood on my lips, smiling at him. He looked like was going to puke "Are you okay?" Nicholas shook his head "I love you." he said before he snapped my neck.

I awoke slowly, feeling groggy, I groaned a bit as my neck felt sore. I slowly sat up, stretching my neck, rolling it around a bit and wincing at how tender it felt "Jesus.." I muttered. I swung my legs to sit on the side of the bed, trying to remember what all happened. My memory was a little foggy, as I sat there trying to figure it all out. I sighed, as I stood up and made my way slowly through the apartment. Lucy and Nicholas were sitting on the couch, talking "Hey.." I said weakly. Nicholas jumped up quickly and he was at my side "Hey..How are you feeling?" he asked me as we got to the couch and sat down "Sore. Weird. I don't know. Off?" I said laughing as I shrugged my shoulders. Lucy laughed "Well, I bet your neck really feels sore. He snapped your neck hard." she said, shaking her head, I gaped at her before looking at Nicholas "You did what?" I was in shock. Nicholas sighed "I told you I didn't want to do it. You have to die to turn. Snapping your neck was the quickest was." he said, looking very sad and upset. I smiled sweetly at him, reaching out to cup his face "Thank you." I told him, as I kissed him, he kissed me back and I felt my hormones rush with excitement, I wanted him so badly. He laughed against my lips, as he pulled away some "Calm down. Everything is going to be super heightened for the next month until you can control them. Especially with hunger." I nodded my head "But I promise, I will be there with you through it all." He kissed my forehead "I will too!" piped in Lucy "We've got you, Abby!" I smiled and laughed. I had my brand-new family. Though things were going to be rough for the first month of this whole new process, I knew I had Nicholas and Lucy to help me. They would show me the way and how to survive. I couldn't wait to spend the rest of forever with Nicolas as my husband. I couldn't wait to live forever by his side.

www.ingramcontent.com/pod-product-compliance
Lightning Source LLC
Chambersburg PA
CBHW061618130726
47996CB00003B/1021